D0913165

THE BEST THING YOU CAN STEAL

THE BEST THING YOU CAN STEAL

Simon R. Green

SEVERN
HOUSE

First world edition published in Great Britain and the USA in 2021
by Severn House, an imprint of Canongate Books Ltd,
14 High Street, Edinburgh EH1 1TE.

Trade paperback edition first published in Great Britain and the USA in 2022
by Severn House, an imprint of Canongate Books Ltd.

severnhouse.com

British Library Cataloguing-in-Publication Data
A CIP catalogue record for this title is available from the British Library.

ISBN-13: 978-0-7278-9122-8 (cased)
ISBN-13: 978-1-78029-760-6 (trade paper)
ISBN-13: 978-1-4483-0498-1 (e-book)

Typeset by Palimpsest Book Production Ltd.,
Falkirk, Stirlingshire, Scotland.

There is a world beneath the world, where magic and horrors run free, wonders and miracles are everyday things, and the dark streets are full of very shadowy people. You can spend your whole life in the brightly lit streets and never experience anything from this other world. But all it takes is one step off the kerb, into the really fast lane, and suddenly you're living in a much larger world.

Once there, you can never go back. But then, why would you want to?

My name is Gideon Sable, these days.

I'm a thief and a con man, a smooth operator and a bit of a rogue, but never the bad guy. I specialize in stealing the kind of things that can't normally be stolen. Like a ghost's clothes, a radio that lets you listen in on what the dead are saying, or a photo from a country that never existed.

And the people I steal from always have it coming.

Every crime has a victim. The bigger the crime, the more people get hurt. So the trick is to choose the right crime, to hurt the right people. I'm planning a heist, to steal the only thing that matters from the worst man in the world. To get past his security, I'm going to need a crew who can do the impossible. Fortunately, the people I have in mind are pretty impossible themselves. The Damned, the Ghost, the Wild Card . . . and my very pissed-off ex-girlfriend, Annie Anybody. The woman who can be anyone.

I have a plan, a secret weapon and a hidden agenda. If everything goes well, we'll all get what we want. Assuming we don't get killed, of course.

ACT ONE
Putting Together the Crew

ONE

Old Harry's Place
Not a Magic Shop

London is the city where dreams can come true. The good and the bad and the highly unlikely. Which is why I was walking through the narrow backstreets of Soho in the early hours of a cold autumn morning. Old-fashioned street lamps shed a flat yellow glow, like sunlight that had gone off, as I sauntered through an area rich in history and legend . . . and all the other things that lend a misleading lustre to the more unsavoury pastimes.

You don't just stumble across streets like these; you have to go looking for them.

The air was as cold as a banker's heart, and the evening was heavy with a sense of anticipation – of great opportunities lurking round corners, and magic waiting in the wings. I was on my way to steal a bad man's luck and make it my own. Because that's what I do, these days.

I turned the right corner, into the right street, just in time to see a Rolls-Royce come gliding haughtily towards me. I slowed my pace so I wouldn't catch up to it too soon. The long vehicle eased to a halt with the air of an aristocrat deigning to visit the less fortunate. Sir Norman Powell was something in the City, an iron-willed tyrant who ran his business empire as though slavery had never gone out of fashion. Normally, he wouldn't lower himself to admit an area like this even existed, but once a week he turned up here for the same reason as everyone else: because he wanted something you can only find in streets like these. Sir Norman might be a strict taskmaster when it came to running his business, but on his own time he preferred the company of the kind of lady who was always in charge.

Sometimes, when he loosened his old school tie, you could catch a glimpse of the leash marks on his throat.

Sir Norman hadn't got where he was today through hard graft, talent or even family connections; he owed it all to charm. A good luck charm, to be exact: the preserved paw of a pookah. Very powerful magic, and very dangerous, because you could never be sure when the pookah might turn up looking for it. But as long as Sir Norman made use of the paw to further his best interests, Lady Luck was always going to be in his corner, cheering him on.

The car door opened and Sir Norman got out. He wasn't much to look at: just another middle-aged man whose Savile Row suit had more style than he ever would. He didn't look round to see if anyone might be watching, because no one he knew would ever lower themselves to frequent an area like this. So he never saw me coming.

I timed it carefully, so I seemed to be just strolling past as he stepped out on to the pavement. I had the ballpoint pen in my hand and hit the button the moment I was in arm's reach. And just like that, Time slammed to a halt. The light around me darkened as it slid down the scale into infra-red, and the air became as thick as treacle. I had to force my way through it, holding my breath because there was nothing to breathe. I slid one hand inside Sir Norman's jacket, forcing aside material that had become as hard as iron, grabbed hold of the white rabbit's paw and pulled it out. The paw seemed almost to nestle into my hand, as though happy to be leaving such an undeserving master. I slipped it into my pocket and hit the button again. Time surged forward and the everyday world returned.

I continued down the street as though nothing had happened, and as far as Sir Norman was concerned, nothing had. Everything I'd done had taken place between one moment and the next, too fast to notice. I smiled as I put my pen away. Just one of the many useful things in my possession that helped to make me such a great thief. How did I get the pen? I stole it, of course.

I knew about Sir Norman's lucky charm because I made it my business to listen in the kind of places where people like to talk. The quiet side-street bars, where the people who work for the people who matter like to congregate when they're off duty. So they can drown their sorrows, forget the day they've had and share their troubles with people who understand. They always end up talking about things they're not supposed to discuss, just because they know they're not supposed to. It's such small rebellions that make their lives bearable. I listened unobtrusively, put the clues together, studied Sir Norman from the shadows . . . and weeks of careful planning paid off in a moment's dexterity and nerve.

I rounded the first corner I came to and hurried down the street. I wanted to be far and far away when Sir Norman discovered his luck was gone. With the paw in my possession, all the bad luck it had been deflecting for so many years would soon come crashing down on Sir Norman – and serve him right. The pookah's paw was a comfortable weight in my pocket, but I had no intention of hanging on to it. Partly because Sir Norman would undoubtedly move heaven and earth to get it back, but mostly because I had more sense than to annoy a pookah. I was on my way to Old Harry's Place to exchange the paw for something far more useful.

You've no doubt heard about those marvellous magical shops that sell wonders and treasures and all the stuff that dreams of avarice are made of. Strange establishments, hidden away down obscure back alleys, that come and go according to their own inscrutable whims. Old Harry's Place isn't like that. It's a pawnshop that's always there and always open. You can find anything you want at Old Harry's Place.

All the other shops on the street were closed, and Harry's darkened window had nothing to show me but my own reflection. I took a moment to admire my new image. Tall, dark-haired and just handsome enough to run most cons, I was wearing a black goatskin jacket, a brilliant white shirt and grey slacks. I don't do colours, these days. I'm making a statement. I nodded to my reflection, and it winked back at me. A small flickering neon sign above the door said simply *Buyer Beware*. The door wasn't locked, because it never is, so I strolled right in, putting on my most confident face.

I paused just inside the door, next to the stuffed grizzly bear, because the shop's interior always takes a little getting used to.

At first, you think it's just a crowded display room, packed with all manner of rare and precious things, until you realize how far back it goes. The stacks and shelves fall away into shadowy recesses that look as if they go on for ever. There are stories about people who've gone in exploring and never come out again. But then, there are lots of stories about Old Harry's Place.

A lot of them concern Harry. Some say he's a demon let out of Hell to tempt people with his matchless merchandise. Others have been known to murmur that he's immortal, and his shop has always been around in one form or another, tricking us into giving up things that matter in return for things that don't. And there are those who say he's the frontman for a weird alien invasion, buying up our culture one crooked deal at a time. Most of us think Harry makes up all these stories so that no one will ever guess who or what he really is.

The only thing you can be sure of with Harry is that no matter how good a deal you think you've made, he's always the one who ends up smiling.

Old Harry's Place is the kind of shop where you can find things you've been searching for your whole life. Where everything you ever lost or cared about or dreamed of is tucked away somewhere, in some dimly lit corner. Harry's shelves are crammed with impossible delights, like the Aladdin's caves we stumble through in dreams, searching for the one elusive item we just know will finally make us happy and content. The air is thick with dust and memories, and the faintest of fragrances, like the ghosts of crushed flowers.

The perfect place to browse guitars that used to belong to dead rock stars, glass display stands offering maps of lost lands, and boxes full of medals from wars no one remembers. You can admire moths pinned to a board, their wings still flapping piteously, or a human skeleton with a steel punch hammered through its forehead. Wonder at a long row of china figurines, depicting all the angels named in the Kabala, or an equal number of deformed candles, representing the Fallen.

Lines of fairy lights hang down from the ceiling, with wee-winged creatures plugged into their sockets, glowing like Christmas decorations. Current junkies. They sang me a pretty song as I threaded my way carefully through the maze of shelves and open bins, heading for the counter.

I didn't see anyone else in the shop, but there could have been any number of people browsing in the far reaches. As always, Harry was perched precariously on his high chair behind the counter, so he could look down on everyone else. A large, square man with a large, square face, Harry was a thoughtful gnomish presence in a suit that looked as if it could use a good dusting. He fixed me with a steady gaze over the granny glasses perched on the end of his nose as I approached the counter.

'Hello, Harry,' I said cheerfully. 'It's been a while, but . . . I'm back!'

'Well, well,' murmured Harry, in his dry, distant voice that was never surprised by anything. 'Look what the night dragged in. Trouble in a black leather jacket, with intrigue on its mind. Hello, Gideon.'

I didn't ask how he already knew my new name; Harry knows everything. I glanced around the shop, doing my best to look unimpressed.

'All the wonders in the world, piled up high and sold for just that little bit more than anyone ever wants to pay. I have to wonder, Harry: what does the vintner buy, one half so precious as the stuff he sells? What do you get out of running a place like this?'

'Job satisfaction,' Harry said calmly. 'What brings you back to me, Gideon, after such a long absence? Could it be I finally have something you can't do without, that you couldn't find anywhere else? Can I tempt you with the teddy bear you loved more than life itself as a child, that your mother threw out? How about the current address of the first girl to break your heart? Or perhaps . . .'

'I'm here to meet Annie,' I said.

'Alas, dear boy, that lady hasn't graced my humble establishment with her presence for even longer than you.'

'She'll be here,' I said. 'But until she arrives, I have a little something you might be interested in.'

'Of course you do,' said Harry. 'No one ever comes in just to chat.'

I reached into my pocket, brought out the pookah's paw and

placed it on the glass countertop. Harry studied it for a long moment, his face giving nothing away, and then he reached under the counter and brought out a heavy steel gauntlet. He slipped it on to his left hand, picked up the paw and put it away under the counter. When he brought his hand back up, the gauntlet was gone. Harry nodded briefly to me, the nearest he could bring himself to appearing pleased.

'Aren't you going to ask me where I got it?' I said.

'You know I never ask questions,' said Harry. 'Because I don't care. You always bring me the tastiest items, dear boy! I've almost got enough parts now to make a whole pookah. You haven't stated a price, which leads me to suppose you're here to make a trade. What is it you're looking for?'

'You know what I want. I want the compass, Harry. The one you said I'd never be able to afford the last time I was here.'

Harry sighed quietly. 'You still can't, but . . . You are a devil, dear boy, to tempt me so unmercifully.'

'I learned it all from you, Harry.'

He reached under the counter and brought out an old-fashioned steel-bound compass. No matter what you ask for, Harry can always produce it from somewhere under the counter. He hefted the compass in his hand for a moment, as though trying to decide whether he could bear to be parted from it, and then placed it carefully on the glass counter. I picked it up, and the needle swung wildly until I concentrated, and then it pointed steadily at the door behind me. I smiled and closed my hand around it.

'This will do nicely.'

'A compass to point the way to whatever you need,' said Harry. 'Do I have to remind you that what you need often turns out to be very different from what you want?'

'I've always been able to tell the difference,' I said.

'Not always,' said Harry. 'Or you wouldn't be here looking for Annie Anybody.'

The compass vibrated in my hand, and when I turned, the door was already opening. A glamorous redhead came through first, wearing too much makeup and a silver lamé evening dress that she still somehow managed to make look cheap. She was hanging on the arm of a large brutal figure in an expensive suit that I just knew he didn't appreciate.

Danny Page . . . businessman, entrepreneur and thug about town. Very definitely married to someone other than the redhead. I quietly put away the compass and stepped back from the counter.

Danny looked disdainfully around the shop. I was pretty sure that was his default expression. His scowl deepened as he looked at me. Whatever had brought Danny to Old Harry's Place, he didn't want any witnesses. I smiled happily back at him, refusing to take the hint, and Danny was lost for a response. He wasn't used to people he couldn't intimidate with a look. The redhead tugged insistently at his arm.

'This is the place I was telling you about, darling! They have the most marvellous things here! And you did promise to buy me something special . . .'

Her voice was high and breathy, and her eyes were really wide, despite the weight of her false eyelashes. The smile she bestowed on Danny would have fooled anyone else, but I knew a honey trap when I saw one.

Danny nodded reluctantly to the redhead and allowed her to lead him to the counter. I fell back a little more to give them some room. Danny glowered darkly at Harry, who merely nodded politely in return.

'Mr Page . . . How may I be of service to such a distinguished gentleman as yourself?'

'I remember this place from when I was a kid,' Danny said slowly. 'We were all too scared to come in here, because of what our parents told us about you. But in the end . . . it's just some-where else I could buy with the small change in my pocket.'

The redhead pouted enticingly. 'But they have such nice things here, sweetie . . .'

She broke off as Harry held up a gun and showed it to Danny.

'You can have this back when you leave, Mr Page.'

Danny looked at him, shocked, and then his hand dived to where the gun should have been and came back empty.

'How did you . . .?'

Harry smiled briefly. 'Do you really want to know?'

Danny thought about it and decided that he didn't. Harry made the gun disappear under his counter. Danny scowled at the redhead.

'What do you want? And make it quick.'

'I want something special, to show how much you love me,' said the redhead. 'You promised me a diamond ring!'

I had to smile. I could see the honey trap closing, even if the mark couldn't. The redhead was working for the wife, looking for hard evidence that her man was cheating on her. A man could lie about the lipstick on his collar, but not about the diamond ring on another woman's finger. Harry reached under his counter, brought out a cardboard box and dumped it on the glass top. It was packed with gold and silver rings, some set with gems that glowed supernaturally bright, charged with such presence they seemed to fill the whole shop. Danny and the redhead stared into the box, mesmerized.

'Rings,' said Harry. 'Invisibility rings, wishing rings, destiny rings; blessed and cursed. My very own lucky dip.'

Danny raised his eyes to look at him. 'Maybe some of the old stories are true after all.'

The redhead was already picking rings out of the box and cooing over them. 'Diamonds are a girl's best friend, sweetie . . .'

'Whereas rubies are the kind of friend who calls you a slut behind your back, so they can steal your boyfriend,' I said cheerfully.

Danny glowered at me. 'You. Disappear.'

'Oh, you just carry on,' I said. 'Don't mind me.'

I moonwalked into the rear of the shop, deep enough into the shadows to conceal me, but still close enough to keep an eye on what was happening. Danny made a move to go after me, but the redhead quickly grabbed his arm.

'Help me choose, sweetie. They all look so lovely!'

Danny looked into the box, and his hand went straight to one particular ring. He held it up to the light so they could both study the heavy gold encrusted with diamonds.

'Ooh . . .' said the redhead. 'I want that one, sweetie!'

'An excellent choice, Mr Page,' said Harry. 'A destiny ring – for the man who's going places. The stones were fashioned from fragments of the Mountain of Light, when Albert had it cut down as a present for Victoria.'

'How much?' said Danny.

'The soul of your firstborn,' said Harry. 'Or the last ten years of your life. Special rings have special prices.'

Danny gaped at him for a moment and then threw the ring back into the box. 'Are you kidding me? This whole shop and everything in it isn't worth that!' He turned on the redhead viciously. 'What kind of scam is this? You're the one who insisted on coming here; what kind of game are you playing?'

'I didn't know!' the redhead said quickly. 'I'll choose another ring, sweetie – something you can afford.'

That was the wrong thing to say. Danny drew back his hand to hit her. And I hit the button on my pen. Time slammed to a halt, and Harry's shop was suddenly suffused with a harsh crimson light. There was a feeling of dust falling endlessly and the sound you hear between heartbeats. I came forward out of the shadows, moved in behind Danny and pulled his trousers down. It took some effort to wrestle the rigid materials down around his ankles, and by the time I was done, I was getting dangerously short of breath. I looked at Harry, and he winked at me. Which should have been impossible, but that's Harry for you.

I slogged my way over to the front door and forced it open, and then went back to stand behind Danny. I hit the button on my pen and took a deep breath as Time started up again. Danny yelped with surprise as he saw where his trousers were, and forgot all about hitting the redhead. He bent over to pull up his trousers, and I kicked him solidly in the arse.

Danny cried out and stumbled forward, off balance. He sounded more shocked than hurt. It had been a long time since anyone had dared treat him like that. I kicked his arse again. He staggered on, desperate not to fall flat on his face. One last kick was enough to launch him through the open door and out into the street. I slammed the door shut, turned around and smiled at the redhead.

'Hello, Annie. It's been a while.'

'Not long enough,' she said sharply, suddenly nothing like the airhead she'd been playing. 'How did you manage that?'

'All part of my new role,' I said proudly. 'I am now Gideon Sable, master thief!'

Annie shook her head. 'You always did have more ambition than sense.'

I had to smile. 'You're the one who brought your mark to Harry's. I'm sure the wife would have settled for any old ring.'

She sniffed loudly. 'Danny made a big thing about only getting me the best.' She glared at Harry. 'The prices have gone up since I was last here.'

Harry shrugged. 'He should have made the deal. A ring like that could have made him king of the world – for a time.'

'The ring was for me!' said Annie.

Harry raised an eyebrow. 'You think he would have let you keep it?'

Annie turned her glare on me. 'What are you doing back here, screwing up my life again?'

I raised an eyebrow. 'Ingratitude, thy name is woman. I just saved you from a beating.'

'I could have handled him!'

'Yeah, you probably could,' I said. 'But my way was funnier. Anyway! I'm here to offer you a real job.'

'Of course,' said Annie. 'I should have known you wouldn't just happen to be here at the same time as me. How did you find me?'

'I stole a lucky charm from a scumbag banker, just an hour ago,' I said. 'I came here, and the charm arranged things so you'd be here, too.'

Annie frowned. 'But I talked Danny into bringing me here yesterday . . . long before you stole the charm!'

'I know!' I said cheerfully. 'Freaky, isn't it?'

Annie looked at me suspiciously. 'If you had something that powerful, what are you doing at Harry's?'

'I just swapped it for something far more useful,' I said. 'We need to talk, Annie. I'm putting a crew together, for the biggest heist ever.'

The front door burst open as Danny Page came charging in. His trousers were back where they belonged, and his hands were clenched into fists. Annie moved quickly to stand behind me. Either so I could protect her or so I could soak up whatever violence was heading our way. I got ready to hit my pen again, but Harry just nodded to the stuffed grizzly bear by the door, and it reached out and grabbed hold of Danny. He cried out angrily as the heavy arms closed remorselessly around him, tried to fight his way free and found he couldn't. The bear squeezed hard, until all the fight went out of Danny, and then threw him out on to the street again. The door quietly closed itself. The bear nodded to Harry and went back to being stuffed.

'Thanks, Yogi,' I said. I turned to Harry. 'Is your back room available?'

'Possibly,' said Harry.

I dropped an envelope full of cash on to the countertop, and Harry made it disappear. There's only one back room at Old Harry's Place, but somehow it's always available for the right price.

'Hold everything!' said Annie. 'I'm not going anywhere with you, Gideon, until I get some questions answered.'

'If you want answers, we have to use the back room,' I said reasonably. 'Where we can be sure no one else might overhear them.'

'Privacy is guaranteed, my children,' said Harry, smiling avuncularly at us from his high seat. 'You can say or do anything you like in my back room, confident that no one in this world or the next will be any the wiser. Just head on back and the room will find you.'

Annie made a short exasperated sound and stalked off into the shadows. I hurried after her and we quickly left the regular shop behind. The stacks and shelves appeared to extend away on both sides until we seemed to be walking through a crowded warehouse. As though space itself had expanded, to make room for all the amazing things Harry had accumulated.

We passed by a row of old-fashioned slot machines, and one after another they flashed their lights and rolled their counters, paying off big time in showers of money. The jangling coins piled up on the floor, but Annie just kept going, refusing to acknowledge anything was happening. The machines kept on trying to pay out even after they were empty.

'This is why I've been reduced to working as a honey trap,' said Annie, staring straight ahead so she wouldn't have to look at me. 'Every time I use my gift, it gets harder to shut it down. And sometimes it works whether I want it to or not. Still think I'm what you need for your crew, Gideon?'

'I'll always need you, Annie,' I said.

'You haven't changed a bit. You're still a damned fool.'

A door appeared before us, blocking a narrow passageway

lined with rows of fur coats made from the pelts of extremely rare species. The werewolf came with the head still attached as a hood, the yeti stank to high heaven, and the fur on the chupacabra was still moving. The door swung open as we approached, and Annie strode through without slowing. I gave the coats plenty of room and sauntered in after her.

Harry's back room was so small that only the table and two chairs kept me from confusing it with a closet. No windows, no nice pictures on the walls, and definitely no Wi-Fi. A single bare bulb supplied the only light. Once the door closed behind us, it felt as though we'd been cut off from the rest of the world. An unsettling feeling, even if it was what I was paying for. Harry made his back room available for secret meetings, plots and intrigues, and the occasional human sacrifice, which was why there was always plastic sheeting on the floor. You could say or do anything in this room, secure in the knowledge no one else would ever know. And many had.

Annie sat down on one side of the table, and I sat down facing her. It seemed safest to keep a table between us, considering how we'd last parted. Annie fixed me with her best cold, unwavering stare.

'All right,' she said flatly. 'Let's talk. Starting with: how the hell did you become Gideon Sable?'

'The original master thief is gone,' I said. 'I've taken over the name.'

'You really think you can step into his boots?' said Annie. 'That man was a legend!'

'So am I, now,' I said. 'And as far as anyone else knows, I always was.'

Annie shook her head, hard enough to make the ringlets of her crimson wig dance. 'You always did have ideas above your station.'

'I can remember when you did, too.'

I searched her face for even the smallest sign that she remembered how we used to feel about each other, but it could have been a complete stranger looking back at me. So I met her cold gaze with a calm, businesslike stare of my own. Because I needed Annie to believe I knew what I was doing. And yet . . . I couldn't let it go.

'Are you really still mad at me?'

For a moment, she was actually too angry to speak, and then it all came spilling out.

'Mad at you? Because you ran out on me after our last job – with all the money? I had to disappear into a hole and drag it in behind me, just to make sure no one could find me! I don't hear a word from you in almost five years, and now you have the nerve to pop up out of nowhere and ask if I'm still mad at you? What do you think?'

'I had to disappear,' I said steadily. 'People were looking for me. Someone talked; I never did find out who. I had to vanish completely before they found out about you. The real you.'

Annie sat back in her chair and folded her arms tightly. 'You always did have an answer for everything. But I don't care any more. You're wasting your charm on me, Gideon. I stopped believing in you a long time ago.'

I didn't say anything, letting the silence drag on until she couldn't help but ask the next question.

'What could be so important to bring you crawling out of the woodwork? And what makes you think I want to hear anything you have to say?'

'I'm putting together a very special crew, for a really big heist,' I said. 'I have a patron, funding . . . and the kind of payoff you can retire on.'

She didn't quite laugh in my face. 'Who would hire you for a job like that?'

'Not me,' I said. 'Gideon Sable, master thief.'

'You never learn,' Annie said tiredly. 'Every score was always going to be the biggest, every job a guaranteed success – right up to the point when it suddenly wasn't. Give me one good reason why I shouldn't just punch you in the face for old time's sake, and walk out of here?'

I met her gaze unflinchingly. 'So you can go back to being a honey trap?'

'A girl has to make a living,' said Annie. 'After what you did to me, I had to take what I could get.'

'Then look on this as my chance to put things right,' I said. 'I have a plan, and a victim you'll approve of. Let me give you your old life back.'

'First rule of the con,' said Annie. 'If something seems too good to be true, the odds are it is. What's the catch?'

I grinned at her. 'Are you kidding? We're going to burgle the secret vault of the worst man in the world! The odds are we'll all end up dead!'

She smiled for the first time. 'All right, I'll bite. Who would we be stealing from?'

'Fredric Hammer.'

She sat up straight, her smile gone in a moment. 'Damn you; I'm in. But only as a business partner, nothing more. Is that clear?'

'Of course,' I said. 'Now, what's going on with your gift?'

'You remember how I acquired it,' she said.

I did. Basically, it was a love charm gone wrong. Annie stole the charm because it was so badly guarded it would have been a crime not to, but she didn't have time to find the instructions on how to make it work. So it ended up making machines fall in love with her and want to do anything to please her.

'Everything was fine when my gift could make cash machines empty themselves for me,' said Annie. 'Or persuade computers to tell me all their dirty little secrets. But down the years it's become more and more difficult to control. Which is why I'm reduced to working jobs where I don't have to rely on it.'

'I did wonder why you never made more of yourself after we parted,' I said.

'I thought the same about you.'

I smiled. 'So you did think about me?'

She didn't smile back, but she didn't look away. 'You're a hard act to forget, though God knows I've tried.'

'We always were good for each other,' I said.

'You were always good for yourself.'

'Can't give me an inch, can you?'

She raised a single painted eyebrow. 'Would you?'

'Of course,' I said. 'You know I always have a comeback up my sleeve.'

'All right,' Annie said resignedly. 'What have you been doing since you abandoned me to the wolves?'

'You weren't the only one who lost everything,' I said steadily. 'I've had to be a whole bunch of people in the last few years, none of whom you'd have heard of, and I wasn't happy being any of them. Until I lucked into the chance to become Gideon Sable.'

'Don't try to make me feel bad for you,' said Annie. 'Not after what you put me through.'

I leaned forward across the table. I wanted to reach out and take her hands in mine, but she wasn't ready for that yet.

'We used to be so good at what we did, Annie. Taking on the bad guys and making them pay for all the pain they'd caused. Stealing from thieves, conning the con men, showing them what it felt like to be the victim. This is our chance to do that again.'

She was already shaking her head. 'We thought we could take on the whole world, but the world turned out to be tougher and crueller than we ever expected.'

'This is our chance to get back in the big time,' I said. 'To prove ourselves, to ourselves. And become incredibly rich in the process, of course.'

'By stealing from the most dangerous and vindictive man in the world?' said Annie.

'Exactly!' I said. 'How can you not want to be a part of that?'

'All right,' said Annie. 'I know you're just dying to tell me. How did you end up as Gideon Sable?'

'You know how it is,' I said. 'One thing leads to another, and occasionally to something entirely unexpected. Like the location of Gideon Sable's safe deposit box. It took me a while to work up the courage to go after it. I couldn't believe it wasn't a trap. But in the end, it couldn't have gone more smoothly. Like it was meant to be. Like fate had chosen me to be Gideon's successor.'

Annie rolled her eyes. 'Come on . . . When have you ever believed in fate?'

'I believe in making my own luck,' I said. 'When I opened that safe deposit box, I found the secret to Gideon's success. A skeleton key that can open any lock. And this.' I took out my pen and held it up before her. She looked at it politely.

'It's a ballpoint pen, Gideon. They've been around for ages. You must have noticed.'

'No,' I said. 'It only looks like a pen.'

'All right,' said Annie. 'What does it do?'

I grinned. 'You've already seen what it can do. Danny Page never saw me coming.'

She studied the pen with new interest. 'It can make you invisible?'

'Better than that,' I said. 'It can stop Time. For a few seconds. Long enough for me to do all kinds of useful and interesting things.'

'Why just a few seconds?'

'Because there's no air to breathe,' I said. 'So I can only stop Time for as long as I can hold my breath. And . . . there was a note that came with the pen that said, "Don't use it too often. They'll notice."'

'Who are "they"?' said Annie.

'No idea,' I said. 'That's what makes it so worrying.'

Annie started to reach for the pen, but I put it away. I wasn't ready to trust her that much.

'How does it work?' said Annie.

'No idea.'

'Haven't you tried taking it apart to find out?'

'No,' I said. 'Some of us remember the goose that laid golden eggs.'

'Fair enough,' said Annie. 'But why would Gideon Sable leave his most powerful tools in a safe deposit box?'

'Either they were duplicates or he had good reason to believe he might not be coming back from his last job. And, of course, he didn't.'

Annie nodded. 'Was there anything else in the box?'

'Oh, yes,' I said. Smiling again, because I just couldn't help it. 'Something that makes this whole heist possible.'

Annie leaned forward for the first time, interested in spite of herself. 'What? What did you find?'

I sat back in my chair. I had her.

'A book. Containing all the information we need to get past all of Hammer's defences and protections, and inside his private vault. Which, by all accounts, contains the largest collection of weird and unique items ever gathered together in one place. Things so rare you can't buy them for any amount of money; you have to pry them from the cold, dead hands of their previous owners.'

'That's not possible!' said Annie. 'Hammer had that vault specially designed to keep out people like us! How can any book—'

I raised a hand to stop her. 'No more details, Annie. Not till we're alone.'

She frowned. 'No one's listening. Harry guarantees our privacy.'

'But what about Harry?'

'You don't trust him?'

'He's a demon from Hell!'

'Possibly,' said Annie. 'It doesn't mean he's a bad person.'

'This is too big a deal to risk,' I said. 'You can hear the details after I've assembled the rest of the crew.'

'You're asking me to trust you?' said Annie.

'You don't have to trust me. Trust the job.'

She looked at me for a long moment. 'You really think we can rob Fredric Hammer and get away with it?'

'If we do this right,' I said. 'With the right crew.'

'We never needed a crew before.'

'We never went after anything this big before.'

'I liked it when it was just us against the world,' Annie said quietly. 'We were going to be modern-day Robin Hoods, sticking it to the bad guys. Those were good days . . .'

'This heist isn't just about the money,' I said. 'It's our chance to be the kind of people we always wanted to be.'

'I would like to be able to trust you again,' said Annie. 'Who else do you want for this crew?'

'The Damned,' I said.

Annie almost jumped out of her chair. 'Are you crazy? He's a complete bloody psychopath! He kills people! People like us!'

'He'd much rather kill Hammer,' I said, keeping my voice calm and collected because one of us had to. 'The Damned will work with us, just for a chance at Hammer.'

'What do you need the Damned for?' said Annie, scowling hard to make it clear that while she might be curious, she wasn't even a little bit convinced.

'Muscle,' I said. 'Hammer has his own private army of extremely well-armed guards.'

Annie nodded slowly, conceding the point, but she was still frowning. 'Who else?'

'The Ghost,' I said.

'Yes, that makes sense.'

'And one other person,' I said, choosing my words carefully. 'We're going to need the Wild Card.'

Annie honestly couldn't speak for a moment, and then she let me have it, full blast.

'*Johnny Wilde?* Are you kidding me? He's crazy! I mean, *really* crazy! And scary with it. You never know what he'll do.'

'That's the point,' I said. 'With him on our side, no one will be able to predict what we're going to do.'

'You can't trust him,' Annie said flatly. 'That man is a danger to himself and everyone around him.'

'My plan depends on having him with us,' I said. 'Doing what he does best.'

'Like what? Confuse people to death?'

'Something like that,' I said. 'Don't worry, Annie. If he should start getting out of hand, the Damned will be there to shut him down.'

Annie took a deep breath and let it out slowly. 'All right. Just . . . keep Wilde away from me.'

'No problem,' I said. 'Where are you living these days, Annie? I tried all your old haunts, and no one had heard of you in ages.'

'I'm someone else now,' she said. 'Someone Fredric Hammer doesn't know exists. Don't screw up my life again, Gideon. It's all I've got.'

'Your life is safe with me,' I said.

'I wish I could believe that.'

She gave me her new address. It was in a particularly shabby part of town, but I didn't comment.

'We'll all get together at your place, seven o'clock tonight,' I said. 'I will then explain the details of my amazing plan to everyone, and bask in your admiration.'

'Why does it have to be my place?' said Annie.

'Because you're so far off the radar. No one will think to look for us there. Anyway, my place is a mess.'

She smiled briefly. 'It always was.'

'What can I do?' I said. 'I live there.'

'What if one of them turns you down?' said Annie.

I gave her my best confident smile. 'They won't. They all have good reason to want revenge on Fredric Hammer.'

'Aren't you worried I might sell you out to him? He'd be bound to pay good money for information like this.'

'You have more reason to hate him than any of us,' I said. 'He screwed up my life, but he ruined yours. When he told everyone your real name.'

She suddenly looked older and very tired. 'So . . . you did know.'

'I did everything I could to protect you,' I said.

'We should never have gone after that damned Masque,' she said bitterly. 'I told you it was out of our league!'

'You didn't tell me you surrendered your real name to get close to the Masque's owner,' I said.

'It was the only way. When Hammer got to the Masque of Ra first, he acquired my real name as well. And then he told everyone – just because he could.'

'This is your chance,' I said steadily, 'to make Hammer pay for everything he took from you.'

'So this isn't just a job,' said Annie. 'It's revenge.'

I grinned. 'Is there anything better than mixing business with pleasure?'

'You haven't changed a bit,' said Annie.

TWO
Going Underground
All the Way Down

L ondon is a city of levels. Commerce above and transport below, and darker things further down.

Victoria is one of the oldest Tube stations in London and holds many secrets close to its chest. The escalators took me as far down as they could, with early-morning commuters packed in around me, bleary-eyed and scowling at the prospect of the day ahead. I left them behind as I descended past the regions they knew to arrive at a side door most people can't see. Unless they pay the annual subscription. I carefully pronounced a few words in a language no one speaks any more, and the door swung back, revealing nothing but darkness. I already had my torch ready, and its beam pushed back the gloom as I made my way down the dusty stone steps.

Not many people come this way. Because they've got more sense.

The steps ended at a jagged hole in the wall, halfway along an abandoned railway tunnel. I didn't like to think too much about what might have made the hole. I stepped carefully through, and my torch's narrow beam revealed just enough of the curving walls and roof to add to the claustrophobia of being alone, in a tunnel, deep underground. The air was stale, and the quiet had a weight and a presence all its own. I took out my new compass, and the pointing needle reassured me I was headed in the right direction. I put it away and set off down the tunnel.

Almost immediately, I heard soft furtive sounds, from somewhere off in the dark. I told myself it was just rats and wished I could believe that. I had enough to be scared about, heading into the depths of the underworld to meet with the Damned, because the Damned is seriously scary. When he isn't out killing people he thinks need killing, or doing terrible things for the greater good, the Damned makes his home in a disused Underground station. Because he knows he doesn't belong in the light any more.

There are forty-three Underground stations no longer in use. Replaced by more modern lines or sold off to some of the more secret organizations. People travelling London's thoroughfares would be surprised by some of the things that need to be transported deep underneath the city, for reasons of safety and security. But a few Tube stations were shut down simply because they became too dangerous. Like Hob's Court, in 1940.

During the Second World War, many Underground stations were used as bomb shelters, but no one ever looked for shelter in Hob's Court. People heard things. Some saw things. Passengers had been known to disappear right off the platforms. And once, it was said (or more often whispered), a train arrived at the station after Hob's Court with no one left aboard. Blood gushed out of the carriage doors when they were opened, and the interior walls were slick with gore and bits of splintered bone.

After that, Hob's Court was written off. No one had time to investigate; there was a war on. The entrance tunnels were bricked up, to keep whatever was in there from getting out, and everyone did their best to forget there had ever been a station called Hob's Court. But there are still ways to get there, for those determined enough to brave the things that lurk in the surrounding tunnels.

I'd been this way once before, to talk with the Damned.

It wasn't that difficult to track him down; even people who choose to live completely off the grid still leave a trail through their interactions with other people. The Damned's interactions consisted mostly of sudden death and bloody violence, and he never bothered to hide any of it. I knew I had to talk to him face to face if I was to convince him to do what my client wanted, so down into the underground I went. Whistling cheerfully in the dark tunnels, because I thought I was the only one down there.

I found the Damned sprawled in a deckchair in the middle of the platform, staring at nothing, his grim countenance fitfully illuminated by the crimson light from a single iron brazier. Just a big man in a shabby suit, with a face that looked as if it had been chipped out of stone. I introduced myself with one of the names I was using at the time, and he didn't even look round.

'I chose this place so people wouldn't bother me.'

His voice was low and harsh, little more than a growl. I started to tell him about my client, and suddenly he was standing before me, one hand crushing my throat. He lifted me into the air, my feet kicking helplessly.

'How did you find me?'

'I know things,' I gasped. 'I find people. It's what I do.'

I was finally able to convince the Damned that I was harmless, because I was, and that the person my client wanted him to kill was quite definitely someone the Damned would want to kill. More importantly, only my client could make the kill possible. The Damned's hand closed around my throat, cutting off my voice while he thought about it. Blood hammered in my head as I fought for air. And then the Damned let me go, and I dropped on to the platform, shuddering and gasping for breath. He could have killed me, and both of us knew it.

I sorted out the details of the deal and then ran all the way home. I told the client the job was on and to forget he ever knew me. I comforted myself with the thought that at least I'd never have to face the Damned again.

But here I was, walking along the same tunnel to try to talk the Damned into something else. Only this time I knew what was down in the dark with me. Rather than think about that, I concentrated on what I'd heard about the Damned.

When you know, beyond any shadow of a doubt, that you are damned to Hell for all eternity, you can do anything. Because there's no reason not to. The Damned decided to become the scariest agent for the Good that the Good ever had – and no, the Good didn't get a say in the matter. When he's not busy killing people who deserve to die, the Damned deals in supernatural crime. If your computer is possessed, if the old photos in your family album have started whispering threats, if your guardian angel is spying on you for someone else . . . then the Damned will put a stop to it.

He doesn't do it for payment, or to buy his way out of Hell by performing good deeds. He knows it's too late for that. He just does it to piss Hell off, in one last act of defiance.

From up ahead came the sounds of a party. Laughter and singing, raised voices and raucous behaviour, along with half a dozen different kinds of music. I rounded a long, curving corner and there was Hob's Court, bathed in a familiar flickering light. Home to the Damned and his guests.

I turned off my torch and put it away, gathered up my courage and strode determinedly toward the platform like a neighbour who'd come to complain about the noise.

When I hauled myself up on to the platform, the first thing that hit me was the smell. The stink of too many bodies packed together in one place, and all the aromas of sin: sex and drugs, pleasure and pain, blood and death. Men and women crowded the platform from one end to the other, dancing as if there was no tomorrow, partying till they dropped. Dead bodies had been piled up at the far end of the platform, where they wouldn't get in the way.

There was a frantic desperation to it all, of people determined to have a good time in spite of everything. Some were fashionably dressed, while others wore nothing but sweat and blood. Laughing, singing and crying hysterically, they leapt and swayed to the pounding music, or humped each other on the ground or up against the wall. I saw bare feet slam down on broken glass and discarded needles, but none of them gave a damn.

The only illumination came from the single iron brazier in the middle of the tracks. A dull reddish-orange glow, like light that had spoiled and gone off. An unhealthy light. The flames flared up occasionally, and then the people's shadows danced even more madly than they did.

The party came as something of a surprise. Everything I'd heard about the Damned suggested he'd moved beyond normal human needs and appetites. I searched the heaving crush of bodies, but couldn't spot him anywhere. And then he came striding through the crowd, barging people out of his way as he headed straight for me. A huge brutal figure, with broad shoulders and a barrel chest, the Damned wore nothing but a pair of faded jeans and two silver bands around his wrists. His hairy torso shone with sweat from the heated atmosphere. His eyes were cold, and his mouth was a thin flat line. He had the look of a man who feared nothing, because everything in the world would only break against what he was now.

A man with all the last traces of humanity scoured out of him. Or possibly discarded as not needed any more.

I opened my mouth to remind the Damned who I was. He grabbed a handful of my shirtfront, lifted me off my feet and slammed me back against the wall. He thrust his face forward, his cold gaze boring into mine.

'I heard you coming.'

'Over all this racket?' I said, doing my best to appear entirely unimpressed.

'This is my domain. Nothing happens around me that I don't know about.'

'Then why don't you clean the place up?' I said. 'Teenage boys wouldn't lower themselves to live in a shithole like this.'

He didn't smile, but he did let go of me and step back. 'What do you want? I don't like unexpected visitors.'

'You don't like anyone,' I said. 'Aren't you worried this much noise will draw your enemies to you?'

'Let them come,' said the Damned. 'We're running low on snacks.'

He might have been joking, but I wouldn't have put money on it. I took a moment to tug my rumpled shirtfront back to where it should be and then gave the Damned my most confident look. The one that suggests you really need to hear what I have to say.

'Come on,' I said. 'You remember me. You didn't kill me the last time I was here, so you're not going to kill me now. Not while I can be of use to you. How long has all this been going on?'

The Damned shrugged. 'Weeks. Months. They come and they go, but there are always more.'

'I suppose they're company.'

'They're scum,' said the Damned. 'Attracted to my legend like moths to a flame. Or like a suicide to a razor blade.'

'So why put up with them?'

'They help distract me from my memories,' said the Damned. He looked around him, entirely unmoved by the spectacle of desperate people doing desperate things in pursuit of something like pleasure. 'I suppose Hell will look something like this when I finally get there.'

His gaze fell upon two entwined bodies lying on the edge of the platform. They'd been dead for a while. The Damned put one bare foot against the dead man and woman, and shoved them off the platform and on to the tracks.

'You see?' he said. 'I can be house-proud.'

None of his guests stopped partying. Presumably, they'd seen him do worse things. The Damned fixed me with his cold, unwavering gaze.

'I told you not to come back.'

'I'm famous for not listening to good advice,' I said. 'I'm here to offer you something you need.'

'I don't need anything.'

'Not even a chance for revenge on Fredric Hammer?'

The Damned paused for a moment, as though that was the one response he hadn't been expecting.

'No one can get to Hammer,' he said finally, but his eyes were curious.

'I can,' I said. 'With your help. Want to talk about it?'

The Damned turned away and walked straight into the heaving crowd. He struck out at them with no warning, heavy open-handed blows that sent men and women staggering. They cried out, scattering before him like panicked birds. None of them protested or even tried to defend themselves, as the Damned drove them the length of the platform, kicking them in the arse when they didn't move fast enough. A few he picked up bodily and threw off the platform on to the tracks. His guests fled before him, screaming and crying. Some stopped to pick up their clothes, some didn't. They jumped down from the platform and ran off along the tracks, disappearing quickly into the dark of the tunnel mouth. The Damned came back and kicked the various music machines to death, and a sudden silence fell across the platform.

'That's more like it,' I said cheerfully. 'We can hear ourselves think now.'

'You say that like it's a good thing,' said the Damned. 'What's the plan?'

'Complicated,' I said. 'And I'd rather not go through all the details until the entire crew's been assembled. The point isn't what we'll be stealing or how we're going to do it; the point is to hurt Hammer. And that's what you want more than anything, isn't it?'

'Fredric Hammer is very hard to get to,' said the Damned. 'He's turned his home into a fortress, with all the rarest materials stored in a private vault.'

'I didn't think anyone could stop you,' I said.

The Damned's smile was a quick and humourless thing. 'Hammer made deals with Powers and Forces to protect his precious collection. He has weapons that might even be able to kill me if I was foolish enough to give him a clear shot. And I'm not ready to die, just yet.'

Of course not, I thought. *You know what's waiting for you.*

'Allow me to sweeten the deal,' I said. 'Hammer recently acquired a very interesting new drug: the Santa Clara Formulation. Immortality guaranteed, from a single dose. It's supposed to be based on materials harvested from Methuselah's corpse, but you can take that with as many pinches of salt as you like. What you need to consider is that a man who's never going to die has nothing to fear from the Hereafter.'

'How do you know what Hammer's got in his vault?' said the Damned. 'He never talks about what he has, not even to boast to other collectors.'

'How I know things like that is part of what I'm bringing to the table,' I said.

'Do you have someone inside his organization?'

'In a way.'

He didn't say anything for a while, just stood there with his eyes half closed as he considered the matter, but I could tell he was tempted. I'd baited the hook and he'd bitten, just as I'd known he would. Sometimes I'm so good I scare myself.

'Let's be clear,' I said finally. 'All I'm offering is a chance to hurt Hammer by stealing his most prized possession. You won't get to kill him, because the success of my plan hinges on no one knowing we were ever there.'

'You're worried I might put the job at risk by trying to kill Hammer,' said the Damned.

'Well, wouldn't you?'

'I would risk what's left of my soul for just a chance,' he said.

'I'm not sure even you could kill Fredric Hammer,' I said carefully. 'Like you said, the man has serious protections.'

'Not from me,' said the Damned. He showed me his brief smile again. 'Why do you think no one's seen Hammer in public for so long? He's holed up in his fortress so I can't get to him. He thinks he can wait me out.'

'Would you risk certain revenge on Hammer just for a chance at killing him?'

He thought about it. 'I want revenge. Death can come later. What matters is that he suffers.'

'Are you in or not?' I said. 'Trust me; you won't regret—'

He stopped me with a look. 'I regret so many things. One more won't make any difference.'

'Look,' I said. 'I can't keep thinking of you as the Damned, and I'm certainly not calling you that when I introduce you to the rest of the crew. Makes you sound like a masked wrestler. What's your name?'

'To know a man's true name is to have power over him,' said the Damned. 'You should know that, Gideon Sable.'

I looked at him sharply. 'How did you know I'd taken on a new identity?'

'I hear things. Even down here. You can call me Lex Talon. It's short for *lex talionis* – the law of retribution, where the punishment fits the crime.'

'Disturbing, but fitting,' I said. 'Are you in, Lex?'

'Yes,' he said. He studied me for a long moment, and for the first time I had no idea what he was thinking. When he finally spoke, there was something almost human in his voice. 'I feel I owe you something. Would you like to know the truth about how I damned myself?'

I nodded quickly. I'd heard all kinds of stories, but I didn't think anyone knew the whole truth, except the man standing before me.

'A sign of trust between us, then,' said the Damned. 'With the understanding that if you ever try to tell anyone else, I'll kill you. Do you still want to know?'

'I always want to know,' I said. 'Tell me everything.'

And he did.

THREE

The Damned

In His Own Words

As with so many awful things, said the Damned, it all started with Fredric Hammer.

He hired me to murder two angels and steal their halos, so he could add them to his collection. He chose a complete amateur because any professional thief would have told him to his face that what he wanted wasn't possible. Hammer's solution to the problem was typical of the man: find someone sufficiently motivated they wouldn't care that the job was impossible.

How do you kill an angel and take their halo? By going to the one place in the world where a truce exists between Heaven and Hell, and angels and demons manifest on a regular basis. Given material bodies for the occasion, with physical limits and weaknesses, so they could properly appreciate the mortals they would be discussing. Unlike any normal, sane human being, Hammer wasn't impressed or intimidated by this; he merely saw an opportunity.

Before I was damned, I was a different person. A minor historian in a minor university, specializing in arcane religious texts. The phone rang one day, in my pokey little office, and when I picked it up, the voice on the other end said Fredric Hammer wanted to meet me. The voice made it sound less like a request and more like an imperial command, but I was assured that Mr Hammer would make it worth my while.

Anyone else I would have turned down. I had a lot of work to do. But the name intrigued me. I'd heard of Fredric Hammer's legendary collection of rare and unusual historical items. So I agreed to the meeting, hoping that, once inside his home, I would be able to talk him into letting me see his collection. But the address I was given was for a hotel in London, at eight in the evening the very next day. The voice didn't say, *Don't be late*. That was understood.

Of such small temptations are lives destroyed.

I travelled to London by train, wondering all the way what a man like Hammer could want with someone like me. What could I know that Hammer would be interested in? The address turned out to be a cheap hotel in a worn-down area. The man at reception didn't even look up from his magazine as I entered the lobby, so I made my way up the stairs to Room 26 and knocked hesitantly on the door. A voice instructed me to enter.

My first view of Fredric Hammer was of a large man in his late sixties, casually but expensively dressed, standing in the centre of the room like the lord of all he surveyed. He had a commanding presence, a predator's smile and cold, cold eyes. All designed to make me feel very much the nobody I was.

He didn't offer to shake hands. I started to introduce myself and he cut me off.

'I know who you are. I've been waiting for you.'

The assurance in his voice made me feel as if I was late, even though I knew I wasn't. I started to apologize and then stopped myself. I couldn't let him walk all over me. I gestured at our humble surroundings.

'Why are we meeting here?' I said. 'What is a man like you doing in a dump like this?'

From the look on his face, I gathered Fredric Hammer wasn't used to being questioned, but he made an effort to appear courteous. Confirming what I already suspected, he wanted something from me.

'I have enemies,' he said shortly. 'I chose this hotel because no one would expect to find me here. You needn't worry; I have security guards in place.'

I frowned. 'I didn't see any guards.'

'You wouldn't,' said Hammer.

'Why am I here?' I said. 'Why did you choose me?'

'I didn't. I have people to do that sort of thing for me. Anathea!'

I jumped just a little as he raised his voice, and then looked round quickly. The door was already opening, as though someone had been waiting to be summoned. A tall, elegant blonde entered the room. Extremely good-looking in a smart business suit, entirely professional in her manner and carrying a briefcase.

'This is my personal assistant,' said Hammer. She took up a position beside him. Hammer didn't even glance at her. 'You can speak freely in front of Anathea. She knows all there is to know about the matter at hand.'

'What matter?' I said. 'You still haven't told me what you need me for.'

'I want the halos of two particular angels for my collection,' he said, as casually as though we were discussing nothing more important than a few rare stamps. 'I have been told you can make that possible.'

'But . . . it's not possible!' I said and then stopped abruptly as I realized I'd raised my voice. Hammer was frowning.

'You recently came into possession of a very interesting document,' he said. 'Giving details of a meeting at an inn in Londinium, in 29 AD. Tell me about it.'

And I was so shocked and startled he knew about it that it never occurred to me not to.

It all began with a crate of old papers I bought at an auction. I was hoping it might contain documents about a schism in the early English Church that I'd been researching. But among many yellowed and crumbling pages of no real worth, I was surprised to find a document from the Dead Sea Scrolls, translated into Latin. It had been dismissed as simple apocrypha and forgotten. Later, I wondered if it had been deliberately suppressed.

The more I studied the document, the more convinced I was of its authenticity, and the more fascinated I became with the story it told. Particularly when the details it gave concerning the inn's location were sufficient for me to track down its modern setting. The inn was still there, almost two thousand years later.

In 29 AD, Joseph of Arimathea visited Britain as part of his interest in the tin trade. He brought with him his nephew, Jesus.

They travelled the country together and finally ended up in the small Roman city of Londinium. They visited an inn, dined and drank wine, and then Jesus announced that he would not be returning home once the business trip was completed. His time travelling with Joseph had given him a taste for exploring the world. He wanted to go to other lands and meet all the different people. Joseph argued that Jesus had to return, because, as the Chosen One, the fate of all Humanity rested on what he was going to do. Jesus disagreed. And while they were discussing this, a woman sat down at the table with them.

She said her name was Rachel and that she represented the Other Side. But to Jesus' surprise, she also insisted that he needed to return home. His life and death were going to be the opening shot in a Great War between Heaven and Hell, for the souls of all Humanity. And Hell couldn't wait to get started because they were convinced they were going to win.

In the end, Jesus would only agree to return if both sides made a pact: that once a year, at midnight, Heaven and Hell would each send an emissary to the inn. To try to find common ground and put an end to the war. Joseph and Rachel looked at each other, shrugged and went along with the pact because neither of them thought such a truce would ever make a blind bit of difference.

Jesus smiled at them. 'You have to have faith.'

When I finished, Hammer nodded. 'I've heard the story before, from various sources, but never in such detail. And you know where the inn is.'

'The inn may be real,' I said. 'But it's still just a story.'

Hammer smiled for the first time. 'No. I have proof.'

He gestured to Anathea, who opened her briefcase and handed me an ancient document sealed in plastic, written in a form of Latin I wasn't familiar with. It took me a while to puzzle out the meaning, and then a chill ran through me as I realized I was reading the contract Jesus had insisted on, to bind Heaven and Hell to the deal. I reached the bottom of the page, and my breath caught in my throat as I took in the three signatures. Joseph of Arimathea, Rachel of Ramah, and . . . I stared at Hammer.

'Is this really . . .?'

'Yes,' said Hammer, as Anathea plucked the document from my hands. 'The actual signature of Joshua ben David, better known as Jesus, the Christ.'

'So the rumours about your collection are true,' I said numbly.

'Of course,' said Hammer. 'So now I know where angels can be found. All I need is a weapon that will kill them, so their halos can be harvested.'

'You'd kill angels, just to add to your collection?'

He showed me his cold smile again. 'I've done worse. I want you to find a suitable weapon for me. I am prepared to be extremely generous. Name your price.'

'What makes you think I could find such a weapon?'

'You found the inn, didn't you?'

For a while, I couldn't say anything. My thoughts were running wild. I still wasn't sure I believed any of this, but the documents seemed real enough . . .

I met Hammer's gaze squarely. 'I'm not interested in money.'

Hammer raised an eyebrow. 'That would make you unique, in my experience. Perhaps I should put you in my collection. What do you want? If I have it or can get it for you, it's yours.'

'My wife, Barbara, died three years ago,' I said steadily. 'A hit and run. They never did find the driver, so I couldn't tell him he destroyed my life as well. If your collection is everything it's supposed to be, you must have something that can bring the dead back to life. That's my price for a weapon that can kill angels. I want my wife back.'

And Hammer didn't laugh at me or tell me what I wanted was impossible. He just nodded slowly.

'I do have something,' he said. 'But you'd be better off taking the money. I could make you rich beyond your wildest dreams.'

'My only dreams are of Barbara,' I said.

'Very well,' said Hammer. 'But for such a price, I would want you to find the weapon and use it. Kill the angels and bring me their halos, and I will give you back your wife.'

'Why me?' I said. 'Why not use one of your own people?'

'Deniability,' said Hammer. 'I like the idea that it will be your actions and your crime, not mine.'

'You really think you can hide your involvement from Heaven and Hell?'

'You'd be surprised what I have in my collection,' said
Hammer.

I went back to my university, thinking hard all the way. I'd never
been particularly religious, but now I was being forced to believe
in all kinds of things. Back in my office, I used all my resources
and contacts to search for more rare apocrypha, until I came across
a curious account concerning the De'Ath family, in Cumberland.
And finally, in a dusty mansion house library, I found a book
written by Alec De'Ath about his travels in nineteenth-century
Turkistan. It told of a terrible and forbidden armoury, hidden away
in the City of Brass Pillars, and the weapon he found there: the
Iscariot Device. A gun that fired silver bullets fashioned from
the thirty pieces paid to Judas to betray the Christ.
   The only weapon in the world that could kill angels, from
Heaven or Hell.
   I returned to the university, caught up in a dream that seemed
increasingly feverish. I no longer recognized the world I moved
in. I corresponded with increasingly arcane scholars, until at
last I discovered the Iscariot Device was being held in the
Vatican's secret Mageddon Armoury. Along with other weapons
deemed too dangerous for Humanity to know about.
   I phoned Hammer and told him what I'd found. He told me
to meet him in the same hotel room, at the same time the next
day. He hung up before I could ask him how he was going to
pay my price.

When I entered the hotel room, Hammer was standing in the
exact same spot, as though he'd never left.
   'I still didn't see any guards,' I said.
   'Good,' said Hammer. 'That means they're doing their job.
Anathea!'
   His personal assistant entered the room, carrying two small
wooden cases. She held one out to me, and I looked at Hammer.
   'All I needed was the name,' he said. 'After that, my people
acquired the weapon for me.'
   'You have the Iscariot Device?' I stared at the wooden case. It
looked so ordinary to contain such a horror. I made no move to
take it. 'How . . .?'

'Mr Hammer has always been able to suborn people to his will,' Anathea said calmly. 'In this case, by putting pressure on a certain Vatican Cardinal who had loved his fellow man not wisely, but too frequently. He agreed to smuggle the weapon out, in return for our keeping his secret.'

'So all you have to do now is kill the angels,' said Hammer. 'Take their halos and bring them to me, and I will give you what you desire.'

I just nodded. I believed all of this was possible because I needed to believe Hammer could give me back my wife. Nothing else mattered. Hammer gestured to Anathea, and she opened the case to show me a gleaming steel revolver with ivory-inlaid handles.

'The Iscariot Device has taken many forms down the years,' said Anathea, her voice carefully businesslike.

'Take the gun,' said Hammer. 'Get the feel of it.'

I took the Device out of its case and hefted it gingerly.

'I don't know anything about guns,' I said.

'The Device will do most of the work for you,' said Anathea. 'All you have to do is point it in the right direction.'

'I thought it would feel . . . evil,' I said.

'It's just a killing tool,' said Hammer. 'Anything else is in the heart of the one who uses it.'

I put the gun in my coat pocket. It hung heavily at my side, as though reminding me of its presence. Anathea opened the other case. It contained a knife.

'You're going to need this,' she said. 'To cut the halos off the angels after you've killed them. It's the Magdalene Blade – from Mr Hammer's collection.'

'And I want both the gun and the knife back after you're finished with them,' said Hammer.

I took the knife out of its case. Just a standard steel blade and a bone handle yellowed and cracked with age. No carvings, etchings or adornments. Again, I didn't feel anything when I held it.

'Does the knife's name have the same significance as the gun?' I said finally.

'According to the ancient parchment that came with the knife,' Anathea said carefully, 'it wasn't the Roman soldier Longinus who pierced Jesus' side with a spear as he hung on the cross. Mary Magdalene stabbed Jesus with her knife, as an act of mercy.'

'As a result of which,' said Hammer, 'that blade can cut through anything.'

I nodded and put the knife in another pocket. I looked at Hammer.

'When I bring you the halos . . .'

'You get your wife back,' said Hammer. 'Now, the angels will appear at the inn two months and four days from now.'

'I know,' I said. 'I'll be there.'

'We'll be waiting for you here,' said Hammer. 'And when I get what I want, you'll get what you want.'

A taxi delivered me to the right place, in plenty of time. When I entered the inn that was supposed to be almost two thousand years old, I was surprised to find it looked just like any other London pub. People were standing around, drinking and talking, and watching a football match on the television. The layout was exactly as described in the original document, and no one paid me any attention as I made my way to the side door that was exactly where it was supposed to be.

A narrow stairway led me up to the next floor. I started up the bare wooden steps, my heart hammering painfully fast. The stairs brought me to another door, and a room with no windows, no furniture and only bare floorboards. All four walls were covered with line after line of writing, etched deep into the stone. It wasn't in any language I recognized. I think now the lines formed a kind of spiritual Faraday cage, cutting the room off from the rest of the world. So that whatever happened inside it would remain a secret, known only to Heaven and Hell. I closed the door and sat down on the floor to wait.

There was hardly any light, but somehow I could see perfectly clearly. No sound, apart from my own breathing. I had more than enough time to wonder if perhaps it was just a story, after all. But the Iscariot Device still weighed heavily at my side, as though impatient to be used.

I didn't need to look at my watch to know when it was midnight. A great sound struck in my soul, shuddering through me. I scrambled to my feet, looking wildly about me. I could feel the angels approaching, falling and rising into the material world. I could hear the flapping of great wings, like slow thunder.

The angels appeared before me. I'd read as much as I could, trying to prepare myself, but I had no real idea what to expect. Just a vague notion that the angel would be a wonderful being with great feathered wings, a circle of light surrounding his head, while the demon would be all horns and teeth and blood-red skin, with massive batwings. But the angel and the demon were equally beautiful and equally disturbing. They both had the same perfect human form, and their faces were empty of any character I could hope to understand. Their wings were made of blinding light and utter darkness, stretching out to touch the walls. And their halos blazed on their heads like burning crowns – a fierce illumination for the angel, and darkness like a break in the world for the demon. Both angels smiled at me. Perfect love and perfect hatred, equally frightening.

Their sheer presence was staggering, as though they weighed so heavily on the world that they could break it just by walking up and down in it. I wanted to fall on my knees before them, confess all my sins and beg their forgiveness. But then I thought of my wife and found I'd already drawn the Iscariot Device.

I shot both of them in the forehead, the angel and the demon. They didn't even cry out as their heads snapped back and they crumpled to the floor, suddenly stripped of all power and grace. I stood where I was, the gun in my hand, until I was sure neither of them was moving. And only then did I put away the Iscariot Device and kneel down beside the two bodies. I wanted to weep, but what I'd done was too big for that. I felt as if I'd just spat in the face of the infinite.

The wings of light and darkness had disappeared, along with the burning halos, leaving only two human shapes with no hair and no eyebrows, no nipples or navels or genitals – not even any fingernails. I tried to tell myself this meant I hadn't killed anything human, but that just made it worse. All that remained of their halos was a silver circlet around their foreheads, sunk deep into the flesh. I tried to remove the angel's halo, but it wouldn't budge. I took out the Magdalene Blade and forced the tip underneath the circlet. I had to dig and prise and carve the halo away from the angel's head, finally using brute force to tear it from the torn flesh. By the time I was done, I was sweating and breathing hard, my hands shaking from more than the effort. I braced myself and turned to the demon.

I finally put the Blade away and got to my feet. And then I cried out in shock as the halos disappeared from my hands and reappeared wrapped around my wrists. They fitted exactly, and the silver burned coldly against my flesh, like shackles binding me to some unguessable course. I tried to tear them off, but they wouldn't budge. I wondered if I'd have to use the Magdalene Blade on myself before I could present the halos to Hammer.

And then I felt a terrible gaze turning in my direction. Great Intelligences, from Above and Below, were becoming aware that something unprecedented and unforgivable had taken place during the agreed truce. I fled from the room, down the stairs and back through the crowded pub. No one so much as glanced at me. I ran out of the pub and on through the streets, heading for the hotel where Hammer was waiting. I could still feel that terrible gaze trying to find me and failing. I thought the Iscariot Device was hiding me. It wasn't until later that I discovered it was the halos.

I wondered what would happen to the bodies. Would new agents be sent from Above and Below to clean up the mess I'd made? And what did happen to angels when they died? Would their spirits return home, no longer contained by their material forms? Or had the Iscariot Device killed their spirits, too? What had I done?

I kept running, and all through the busy streets of London no one turned to look at me.

In the hotel room, Hammer and Anathea were waiting. They looked up sharply as I crashed through the door.

'Where are my halos?' said Hammer.

I showed him the two silver circlets on my wrists, and he frowned.

'Not what I expected . . .'

'Cut from the heads of dead angels,' I said shortly, as I struggled to keep from crying or laughing. 'Give me my payment, and I'll give you the halos.'

Hammer gestured to Anathea, and she came forward with a

large suitcase. She opened it, and it was packed full of money. I looked at Hammer.

'What's this?'

'Your payment,' said Hammer. 'Enough money for you to make a new life anywhere in the world.'

'I told you, I don't want money!' I said. 'I want what you promised me!'

Hammer laughed at me. 'I don't have anything to bring the dead back to life. And if *I* don't, nobody has. Take the money as a kill fee and give me the halos.'

The Magdalene Blade was suddenly in my hand. Hammer stopped smiling. I advanced slowly on him, and he backed away. Anathea retreated with him, her gaze fixed on the Blade.

'That's my knife,' said Hammer. 'It belongs in my collection.'

'You have no idea what it was like in that room, what I went through to get the halos,' I said in a voice so harsh I didn't recognize it as my own. 'I've put Heaven and Hell on my trail for ever, and you think you can buy me off with money? You want this knife, Hammer? Then come to me and I'll give it to you.'

Hammer started to say something, but what he saw in my face stopped him. He should have known: after killing two angels, a man was nothing. Hammer reached inside his jacket, pulled out a gun and shot me in the face.

The halos flashed up my arms and covered me from head to toe in a moment, like a second skin made of blinding light and terrible darkness, split right down the middle. The bullet couldn't touch me. Hammer slowly lowered his gun, while Anathea made frightened mewling noises. She couldn't even bear to look at me directly.

'Tell me,' I said to Hammer. 'Tell me what this means.'

And he was so shocked and scared that he did.

'The halos armour the angels, so nothing can harm them while they take on material form. That's why I wanted them. Because a man armoured by angels' halos has nothing to fear from any mortal enemy.'

'Why didn't the halos protect the angels from me?' I said.

'Because you had the Iscariot Device,' said Hammer.

I nodded slowly. 'Then there's nothing to stop me from taking my revenge on you.'

Hammer grabbed Anathea and threw her at me. She clung to me desperately, and while I was distracted, Hammer darted past me and ran out of the room. All I could think of was going after him before he got away, but Anathea was still holding on to me and getting in my way. So I cut her open from gut to throat and threw her aside. She sprawled on the floor, unable to scream because her mouth was choked with blood. I didn't care. I was already turning away, to go after Hammer.

I could hear him on the stairs below me, but by the time I reached the lobby he was already disappearing through the front door. I charged out into the street and found it packed with Hammer's guards. Anonymous men in anonymous suits, carrying all kinds of weapons. They saw me in my armour, dripping with Anathea's blood, and every single one of them opened fire on me. For all the good it did them.

Past the guards, I could see Hammer, running for his life. I started after him, and the guards crowded together to block my way. So I cut them down and sliced them open. They died shooting me at point-blank range and clawing desperately at my armour with their bare hands. Blood spurted on the air and ran in rivers down the street. I killed them all and kicked the bodies out of my way as I hurried after Hammer. But the guards had slowed me down enough that when I finally reached the end of the street and rounded the corner, there was no sign of Hammer anywhere. He'd made his escape, and I had no idea where to look for him.

And that was the beginning of my new existence, as the Damned.

FOUR

The Lost Children

The Hungry Ones

'If Hammer had held up his end of the bargain,' said the Damned, 'if he'd actually returned my wife to me, I like to believe I would have gone back to that room at the inn and surrendered myself to whatever was there. For judgement and punishment. There might have been mercy because I did it all for my wife . . . Instead, I damned myself for all time, for nothing.'

Lex stopped talking and turned away, staring off into the darkness. Perhaps so I wouldn't see what was in his face. I looked at the silver circlets on his wrists with a new appreciation, and thought about how much Lex's voice had changed as he told his story – perhaps because he was remembering, just for a while, the quiet academic and scholar he used to be.

'What happened to the gun and the knife?' I said finally.

Lex turned back to me, his face as cold and implacable as ever. 'I put them in long-term pawn, with Old Harry. The one place I could be sure Fredric Hammer couldn't get to them. And the one person I could trust not to be tempted to use them.' He stopped and frowned. 'Always assuming he is a person . . .'

'If I get you your chance to hurt Hammer,' I said, 'will that satisfy you?'

'No,' said Lex. 'But the immortality drug should be enough to keep me going until I can find a way to kill him.'

'And then what?' I said.

'I could live for ever, knowing he was dead,' said Lex. 'Or I could burn beside him in Hell and be content.'

I had no answer to that. But then, he wouldn't have cared if I had. He looked at me thoughtfully.

'You're not the original Gideon Sable.'

'How can you be sure?' I said. 'I could have been.'

'Because I've met him,' said Lex. 'He came down here some time back, to tell me he'd found a way out of my being Damned, and all I had to do was help him steal it from Hammer.' He smiled briefly. 'Everyone thinks they can manipulate me, just by using that name. And, of course, they're right. I told Gideon I was in, but he never came back. And now here you are, offering me the very same deal.'

'I'm not going to disappear on you,' I said steadily. 'And I can deliver what I promise.'

'Then I'm in,' said Lex.

'You don't mind that I'm trading on a dead man's reputation?'

'He's not dead,' said Lex.

That stopped me. 'Then where is he?'

'Trapped in the house where Time stands still,' said Lex. 'He loved the wrong woman.'

'Don't we all?' I said.

He just looked at me.

'Let's be clear about this,' I said. 'If you're going to be part of my crew, I'm the one in charge. Because I'm the man with the plan.'

'I'll follow your orders,' said Lex. 'Right up to the point where I don't.'

I nodded. That was as much as I'd hoped for.

'Find some clothes,' I said. 'I can't be seen with you looking like that. We need to appear professional.'

'There's bound to be something here I can use,' said Lex, looking vaguely round at the discarded clothes littering the platform. I considered the state of most of them and suppressed a shudder.

'Try to find something that doesn't reek of sweat. Or sin.'

'Picky picky,' said Lex.

I gave him Annie's new address and the time to join us that evening.

'Why the delay?' said Lex.

'Because I still have to convince two more specialists to join my crew.'

'Anyone I'd know?'

'The Ghost.'

He nodded. 'That makes sense.'

'And the Wild Card.'

'You be careful around him,' said Lex. 'He's dangerous.'

And then he broke off to stare intently at the tunnel mouth I'd arrived through.

'What is it?' I said quietly.

'You were followed,' said Lex.

'Damn,' I said. 'I thought I'd left them behind.'

'They're not here for you,' he said. 'Another reason for my little gathering was that the constant noise helped keep the Lost Children at bay.'

I strained my eyes against the shadows filling the tunnel mouth, and the darkness stared back at me, giving nothing away. My heart was beating uncomfortably fast. I wanted to get the hell out of there, but I couldn't while the Damned was still standing his ground.

'How many do you think are there?' I said, careful to keep my voice calm.

'More than I've ever seen assembled in one place.'

His gaze was steady, his voice entirely untroubled. I swallowed hard. My mouth had gone dry.

'You can see in the dark?'

'The dark keeps no secrets from me,' said Lex.

'I always thought they were mindless,' I said, just to be saying something. 'Why do they want you so badly?'

'As long as I have the halos, I stink of the Hereafter,' said Lex. 'And the Lost Children want that more than anything, even though they no longer remember why.'

'But they won't come into the light,' I said, trying hard to sound positive. 'They never come into the light. Everyone knows that.'

'Everyone is wrong,' said Lex.

The Lost Children are ghosts that have gone feral. Ghosts of men who died building the Underground system, killed in accidents and cave-ins, left to rot in the dark because it was cheaper than carrying them back to the surface. Ghosts of suicides who threw themselves off platforms in front of trains and found it wasn't the end of their problems after all. Ghosts of homeless people who preferred to die down in the dark rather than suffer the cold indifference of the streets above.

Dead for so long they'd lost all memory of who they used to be, nothing left of them but maddened emotions and brutal needs, the Lost Children roam the world below because they've forgotten there's anywhere else to be. Wearing bodies they made for themselves out of the dirt and grime and dust of the tunnels.

All the Lost Children of London's underground.

Dark shapes started edging forward into the flickering light. Lex laughed suddenly, and it was a flat, ugly sound.

'They really should have known better than to come here.'

He jumped down from the platform and strode along the tracks, and a terrible army boiled out of the tunnel mouth to meet him. No longer human, their bodies had slumped and run like melting candles, because the Lost Children could no longer remember what people were supposed to look like. Grimy and distorted, like smoke grown solid, their overlong arms ended in vicious claws. They had no faces, no eyes or ears, but they all knew where Lex was.

A cold hand closed around my heart as the Damned took on his angelic armour. It didn't so much cover him as replace him – a greater thing overwriting a lesser. The darkness that replaced his left side wasn't just the absence of light but had a horrid presence all its own, while his right side blazed brightly, like the sun come down to earth. Armoured by Heaven and Hell, the Damned threw himself at the Lost Children. And they swarmed forward to meet him.

I didn't move. There was nothing I could do against odds like that, and I was afraid to get anywhere near the Damned while his killing fury was upon him.

He raged among the Lost Children, striking them down and tearing their misshapen bodies apart. He ripped off arms and punched faces so hard the heads exploded, sent dark shapes flying through the air with great sweeps of his arms, and trampled the fallen underfoot. The Lost Children responded with angry cries that sounded more animal than human. And nothing the Damned did stopped them pressing forward.

The Damned laughed happily as claws shattered and dark hands broke against his armour. He tore his way into the heart

of the pack, doing terrible things to them with his angelic strength.
But there were so many of them . . . and every moment more
came pouring out of the tunnel mouth.

One of the Lost Children slipped past the Damned and headed
straight for me. It started to pull itself up on to the platform, a
smoke ghost made solid by the strength of its hatred. Vicious
claws gouged furrows out of the platform, its blank grey face
fixed on me with horrid intent. I took one carefully considered
step forward and kicked it in the face. My foot burst through its
head, sending grit and grime flying in all directions, but the
clawed hands just dug deeper into the platform to hold the body
where it was. I stamped hard on each hand in turn, and they
exploded in puffs of dust. The dark shape fell back from the
platform and on to the rails. The Damned turned his armoured
head to look at me.

'You can't fight them! Get out of here! Run!'

'I won't leave you here to face them alone!'

I didn't know I was going to say that until I did, and I was
surprised to find I meant it. Lex had sworn himself to my cause,
to be a part of my crew. I couldn't just run away and abandon
him. But if I tried to fight at his side, the Lost Children would
tear me apart in a moment. It wasn't as if I had any weapons.

I started to reach for the pen in my pocket and then stopped.
Even if I did bring Time crashing to a halt, what good would
that do? The Lost Children would still be there when I ran out
of breath and had to start Time up again. Just by being what they
were, what they'd made of themselves, they were unkillable. And
then I smiled suddenly, as I remembered the pen wasn't the only
useful tool I'd inherited from the original Gideon Sable.

I reached into a different pocket and brought out a heavy iron
key. According to the notes that came with it, this was the ultimate
skeleton key, able to unlock anything. I dropped down from the
platform, ignoring the dusty shape on the rails that was still trying
to get its head back together, and strode confidently toward the
mass of heaving bodies before the tunnel mouth.

The Lost Children couldn't hurt the Damned inside his armour,
so they'd swarmed all over him, pulling him down through sheer
weight of numbers. He struggled and fought them every step of
the way, but still they dragged him along the tracks to the tunnel

mouth and the darkness that lay beyond. Where, eventually, they would find some way to separate him from the halos they hungered after.

And perhaps after that they would make him one of them.

I walked right up to the seething mass of dark and grimy figures, and held up the key. None of the Lost Children turned to look at me, caught up in their dim swirling thoughts of rage and revenge. They didn't see me as a threat.

Their mistake.

I turned the key sharply in the air as I pronounced the activating word, and just like that the key unlocked the forces holding the ugly shapes together. They exploded one after another, like a series of firecrackers. Dust and dirt scattered in all directions, falling slowly in a grey rain as the Lost Children collapsed back into the grime and dust they came from. Until nothing was left on the rails but the Damned, standing alone before the dark tunnel mouth.

He looked slowly around him, taking in what had happened. His armour disappeared, and a subtle tension was gone from the air, as though an unbearable weight had been lifted off the world. Lex turned to look at me and nodded slowly.

'You stole their shapes from them. Maybe you are a master thief after all.'

'Believe it,' I said cheerfully. 'Well, I must be going now. See you at Annie Anybody's place. Try to clean yourself up a bit first.'

I walked off down the tracks, heading for the other tunnel mouth. I didn't want Lex to see how badly my hands were shaking. Because I really hadn't been sure my marvellous idea would work. Once I was out of the Damned's sight, I started running, and I didn't stop till I'd left the Underground behind me and was back in the sane and reassuring streets of London above.

FIVE

When a Man Is Tired of London, He Is Tired of Life

Or Death

London is a city full of ghosts. Most people can't see them, and the ghosts prefer it that way. They have their own business to be about, and the living would only get in the way.

Once I'd left the Underground, I went looking for shelter in the nearest greasy spoon. The cafe's windows were steamed over, hiding its shipwrecked souls from the hard world outside. At that time of the morning, the place was packed with young mothers, coping with small children and exchanging gossip; out-of-work actors leafing through magazines, quietly hoping to be recognized; and old people making one cup of tea last all morning, just for the illusion of company.

I found a table at the back, where I could keep a watchful eye on the door, and forced down three cups of foul coffee. My hands were so unsteady that I needed both of them to hold the cup. I wasn't sure what had unnerved me most: seeing the Lost Children at last in what passed for their flesh or the way the Damned had torn into them. No man should have that much anger in him, or so much delight in letting it loose. The last thing my plan needed was a loose cannon . . . But I was going to need someone that dangerous, to deal with the kind of things Hammer had put in place to protect himself.

That was what I kept telling myself until my hands stopped shaking and I finally found the strength to get up and go out into the city again, to look for the Ghost.

*   *   *

You can find all kinds of ghosts in London. Everything from wispy shades only just there to complete historical re-enactments. Horrid apparitions that peer out of bathroom mirrors in cheap hotels, encouraging the lost and the lonely to pick up the bottle of pills or reach for the razor blade. Or the last fading remnants of once-famous people, having a hard time believing the world could go on without them. And there are always the killers and their victims, endlessly repeating the most important moments of their lives. If all the ghosts of London could be seen at once, they'd make a fog thicker than any of the old pea-soupers.

I followed my compass to Berwick Street, one of the Ghost's usual haunts. Day and night, the Ghost walks the streets of Soho, going nowhere, looking sadly at the world he can't be a part of any more. He never goes inside any of the buildings. They're full of people living their lives, and he knows he doesn't belong there.

The Ghost is different because he still knows who he is, as opposed to who he used to be. He's still a person, rather than the memory of a man. Though he is starting to lose track of some of the details. I wanted him for my crew because even the most expensive security surveillance couldn't see him – but, really, what crew wouldn't want a man who could walk through locked doors?

I could see him because I have a gift for that sort of thing. I stole it from a medium, years ago. She never passed on what the spirits were saying, because she said it was too depressing. I always had a feeling the gift would come in handy one day. It takes a certain amount of self-control to focus on what I need and keep all the other ghosts out . . . All the strange shapes running wildly in the streets, or crawling up the sides of buildings like insects, or screaming endlessly in the face of what they did on the worst day of their lives.

Ghosts make their own hereafters. But try telling them that.

The Ghost was sitting among a group of homeless people. Most of them can see ghosts, because the homeless are almost as out of touch with the world as the dead. And they're not bothered by ghosts – they have far more important things to worry about.

The homeless are very accepting of the different. They have to be, because all they have is each other.

This particular group was sitting patiently on the steps outside a church, waiting for the doors to open, in the hope of being offered coffee or soup or warm clothing. Putting up with the occasional sermon or well-meant advice was a small price to pay for a little unforced charity.

Some of them passed a bottle of something cheap and nasty back and forth, while others assembled cigarettes from dog-ends they'd found in the streets. Men and women huddled together against the autumn chill, discussing the few things that still mattered to them. Such as what the weather was going to be like, the best begging spots, or which authority figures were useful and which were best avoided. As I approached, one man was telling a story about a woman who kindly presented him with a doggy bag from a very expensive restaurant. But when he looked inside, all he could see was assorted grassy things. The diner was an extreme vegan. The man sniffed loudly.

'I said to her, "What, no chips?"'

They all laughed. The Ghost smiled happily in their midst. He rarely joined in the conversations, but he enjoyed listening. They reminded him of what it used to feel like to be alive. A thin washed-out presence, the Ghost wore the memories of old clothes, little more than vague shapes and smears of colour. His face had shrunk back to the bone, and his wispy white hair drifted restlessly, as though disturbed by unfelt breezes. More an impression of a man than the thing itself.

He was the first to notice me, but once he turned to look in my direction, all the homeless did, too. The Ghost was just curious, but they kept a watchful eye on me because experience had taught them that attention from the everyday world was rarely in their best interests. One man held up a handwritten cardboard sign: *Will Swear For Food.* I stopped a respectful distance away.

'Hello, Ghost. I need to talk to you.'

Some of the homeless stirred protectively, but the Ghost smiled at them reassuringly.

'It's all right. I know him.'

He rose to his feet in a single smooth movement that would have been impossible for anyone living and drifted down the

church steps. Several of the homeless shuddered despite themselves as the Ghost walked through them, because he was colder
than they would ever be. The moment he joined me at the foot
of the steps, they all turned away and resumed their conversations. Because whatever the Ghost and I had to talk about was
none of their business.

'Well, well . . . How nice to see you again,' said the Ghost.
'I hear you're Gideon Sable these days. But then, you've had so
many names in your time. While I have trouble remembering
what's carved on my gravestone. Not that it matters. No one ever
visits it, except me. So, what do you want this time, Gideon?
You know, you only ever come looking for me when you want
something.'

'I could use your help,' I said.

'Of course, of course. Only too happy to be of assistance. I
may have forgotten a few things, but I still remember that I owe
you.'

I once saved the Ghost from a pair of television evangelists
who wanted to exorcize him, live on their show. I was still with
Annie back then, and we worked together to sabotage the broadcast. While the holy rollers prayed loudly over the Ghost's grave,
unaware he was standing right there with them, politely asking
them to keep the noise down, I hacked into the evangelists'
computers. I found what I needed in their private files and gave
it to Annie, who used her gift to charm the television equipment.
It happily interrupted the show to broadcast the evangelists'
personal sex recordings to a fascinated audience. As so many
people said afterwards, *Who knew they'd be into that?* The broadcast shut down abruptly, even though it was reaching record
viewing figures, and the evangelists never bothered the Ghost
again.

'I'm planning a heist,' I said. 'And I could use someone in
my crew who won't show up on even the most sophisticated
security systems.'

The Ghost shook his head. It took his hair a moment to catch
up. 'I don't know, Gideon. I mean, this would involve me doing
things, wouldn't it? I don't really do things any more. I sort of
feel I've left all that behind.'

'No, you haven't,' I said. 'Or you wouldn't still be here.'

He smiled ruefully, acknowledging my point, but he still didn't look convinced.

'What about guard dogs? They'd know I was there. Dogs always bark at me. I don't know why. I like dogs.'

'There won't be any dogs. As such.'

'And I'm not sure about being part of a crew . . . I mean, they wouldn't be able to see or hear me, would they? I don't like being ignored. It makes me feel even more not here than usual.'

'All the people in my crew are as weird as you,' I said reassuringly. 'They'll have no trouble interacting with a ghost. My old girlfriend is one of them; you know her.'

'Oh, Annie Anybody, yes . . . Pity about what happened to her gift.'

I didn't ask him how he knew. He probably couldn't have told me.

The Ghost gave me a sideways look. 'You're not the first person to invite me to join a crew. People always think I'd make the perfect burglar. But I always say no. I'm very busy, after all. These streets won't haunt themselves.'

'The job I have in mind will only take a few days,' I said. 'You'll be in and out before you know it.'

'I won't have to do anything physical, will I?' the Ghost said anxiously. 'I mean, I'm just spiritual. Heavy lifting is beyond me.'

'I only need you to stick your head through a few locked doors and see what's on the other side.'

'Oh, yes, I can do that,' the Ghost said happily. 'In fact, I do it a lot. You don't lose your curiosity just because you're dead.'

'Then you're in?'

'Depends. Who's the target?'

'Fredric Hammer.'

'Oh . . .' said the Ghost. 'You know what he did to me?'

I knew the story; everyone did. But I pretended I didn't, because he did so love to tell it.

'I used to be an art forger,' the Ghost said proudly. 'One of the best. You can still see a lot of my work hanging in museums. Under far more famous names, of course. I was doing very well – lots of money, a quiet kind of fame and all the work I could handle. Until I got the chance to sell Hammer one of my fakes, for his collection. I should have known better, but I never could resist a challenge.

'It was a bloody good Turin Shroud, if I say so myself. I spent ages putting together a credible back story, to explain why the world thought it was still where it should be. Where I went wrong was in taking a short cut with the cloth. Sourcing the real thing would have gouged a huge chunk out of my profit, so I faked it. But the suspicious bastard had it carbon-dated . . .

'With the money Hammer paid me, I could have retired to Hawaii, but I never was one for lounging around on the beach. I only ever felt at home in Soho, so I was still here when Hammer's people came looking for me. I'm told the manner of my murder was so grisly it made the national news. I don't remember it – which is just as well, I suppose.'

He stood staring at nothing for a while and then turned to look at me seriously.

'Are you sure this is a good idea, Gideon? Fredric Hammer is a powerful, vindictive and very dangerous man. I wouldn't want what happened to me to happen to you.'

'My plan is sound,' I said. 'We can do this.'

'Lots of people have said that,' the Ghost murmured sadly. 'But none of them ever come back from Hammer's private vault to boast about it.'

'Let me sweeten the deal,' I said. 'Hammer recently acquired something that could give you a new chance at life. An ancient artefact that would allow you to possess anyone you wanted.'

'Oh, I couldn't do that!' the Ghost said immediately. 'That wouldn't be right. And I wouldn't know how to possess anyone anyway.'

'The artefact would do all the heavy lifting,' I said. 'We're talking about something very special here.'

'You always are, Gideon,' said the Ghost. 'What is it this time?'

I smiled on the inside. He never could resist a good story.

'A long time ago, Jesus forced the demon called Legion out of a man and into a herd of pigs, which then stampeded over a cliff into the sea and drowned. But one of the carcasses drifted ashore, where it was found and harvested for the unnatural energies it still contained. Most of it's been used up, down the centuries, but there is still a single ring, fashioned from a sliver of rib. Slip that ring on someone's finger and it will open a door in their head, allowing you to walk right in.

'The previous owner wore it himself, so he could be possessed by minor demons and do all the appalling things he never had the courage to do on his own. In the end, he went too far. Where else could he go? And Hammer's people took the ring off his corpse.'

The Ghost shook his head firmly. 'Force someone else's spirit out, so I could take over their body? No, Gideon, that's just wrong. But . . . if Hammer should happen to have something in his vault that would allow me to die completely at last, and move on . . .'

I looked at him for a moment. I'd never heard him talk like that before. I suppose even ghosts can get tired.

'If it's there, I promise I'll find it for you.'

'Then I'm in,' said the Ghost.

He stuck out a bony hand for me to shake. I carefully closed my hand around where his appeared to be, and we mimed a handshake. It felt like holding a handful of cloud – cold but indistinct. I gave him Annie's new address and told him when to be there.

'I know it's outside your usual area,' I said.

'Oh, I'm not bound to Soho,' said the Ghost. 'It's just that these are the streets I grew up in. The familiar sights and sounds help hold me together. I like to think that when I finally do move on, Heaven will look a lot like Soho. Where the clubs never close, the bars are full of old friends, and the party never has to end.' He smiled wistfully at the thought.

'It was good to see you,' I said.

'Nice to be seen,' the Ghost said solemnly. 'Who else will be at Annie's place?'

'The Damned,' I said.

The Ghost just nodded, not bothered in the least.

'And the Wild Card.'

The Ghost looked at me sharply. 'You're going after Johnny Wilde? The man who saw too much? Best of luck getting hold of that one. I'd rather chase a poltergeist with a butterfly net.'

He turned and walked away, receding quickly into the distance without covering any ground, growing smaller and smaller right in front of me until I couldn't see him any more. I took a deep breath, braced myself and set off in search of the most disturbing member of my crew. I practised looking calm and confident, because I couldn't afford to appear less than utterly convincing when I talked to Johnny Wilde.

Everyone knew you took not just your sanity but your very existence in your hands when you met with the Wild Card.

SIX

Found in a Graveyard
Talking Loudly

L ondon is a city full of mysteries. A sprawling chaos of streets ancient and modern, where what you see is merely the tip of the iceberg. There are levels and layers to this oldest of cities – the world most people see and its dark mirror image of crooks and crooked business . . . And then there's the London hardly anyone sees: a gossamer-thin realm of magic and miracles, madness and monsters. Most people have the good sense to stick to their own worlds, but there are always a few determined to go exploring and see what there is to see.

Like Johnny Wilde, the Wild Card. The man who saw too much.

So far I'd found the people I needed for my crew easily enough, but I'd always known it was never going to be that simple with Johnny. I tried my special compass, but the needle just spun round and round without stopping, as though confused by someone who could be anywhere and everywhere, all at the same time.

I asked around, in the kind of places where people know things people aren't supposed to know, but no one had heard anything about the Wild Card. They all seemed quite relieved about that. I didn't blame them. It was generally understood that you had to be careful around Johnny Wilde. People who went looking for him tended not to come back. It wasn't that he was malicious, necessarily, just terribly absent-minded about what was inside his head and what wasn't.

Johnny wandered here and there as the whim took him, searching for something that was somehow always just out of reach. Or perhaps he was running and hiding, desperate to stay

out of something else's reach. It was no use asking him. Even
if you could get an answer out of the man, you could guarantee
it wasn't going to be anything helpful.

Finally, a shadowy presence sitting at the back of a poison-
drinking club quietly remarked that something out of the ordinary
was happening at Highgate Cemetery. Someone was disturbing
the dead by saying things to them. So I nodded my thanks to a
man who was no longer there, and headed out across London.

When I finally got to Highgate Cemetery, the huge black iron
gates had been flung wide open. A heavy padlock lay on the
ground, crumpled up like a piece of paper, and the security chains
had been threaded in and out of the iron railings in an intricate
pattern. Pretty good indications that the Wild Card had been this
way.

I stood before the open gates a while, holding on to my courage
with both hands for fear it might bolt. None of my toys or tricks
would help with Johnny Wilde. My only hope was that Hammer's
name would be enough to keep his attention focused long enough
for me to tell him what I had to say. I straightened my back and
sauntered through the open gates as though I didn't have a care
in the world. When you know you haven't got an ace in your
hand or up your sleeve, all that's left is a really good bluff.

Highgate is terribly overgrown these days, with the trees left to
run riot and enough undergrowth spilling out over the paths
to make you long for a machete. Midday sunlight shed a golden
glow over headstones, monuments and ivy-wrapped columns,
while a host of rather self-conscious-looking angels stood around
making semaphore signals to each other. A few wisps of mist
curled around the headstones, as though they felt someone should
be making an effort. It was all very peaceful, the only sound the
crunch of my feet on the gravel path.

The autumn air was cold and sharp, and everything in the
cemetery looked very real and very solid. It was important to
cling on to thoughts like that around Johnny Wilde.

After a while, I heard a voice in the distance, talking calmly
and reasonably, so I went in search of it. I found Johnny sitting
on top of a cracked tombstone, deep in conversation with a whole
group of people who weren't there. A stout middle-aged man in

a battered tweed suit with leather patches on the elbows, Johnny had a round face, kind eyes and a constant air of distraction – as though far too many things were vying for his attention. He looked like a retired professor. Because he was.

I stamped my feet loudly on the gravel, to make sure Johnny knew I was getting closer. It didn't do to catch him by surprise. But he just kept on talking to all the people I couldn't see. I finally understood from his half of the conversation that Johnny was talking to the occupants of the graves set out around him.

'Well, sir, don't think of it as being trapped in a coffin; think of it as refuge from the noisy and intrusive world. And yes, dear lady, I quite agree it's a shame that your family doesn't visit more often, but at least you're enjoying some peace and quiet. No, young man, I can't do anything about your being buried upside down. What difference would it make? The view wouldn't change. What was that, madam? Oh . . . the whole Heaven and Hell bit. I'm really not the right person to talk to about that. I think you're supposed to let go of this world and take a leap of faith. But I could be wrong. I often am.'

Johnny Wilde could see and hear all kinds of things that the rest of us mercifully can't. That was why I wanted him. If Hammer's place was protected by unknown Forces and Powers, I needed someone on my crew who could see them. Of course, not everything Johnny saw was actually there. It was entirely possible that he was completely mad. General opinion on the matter was divided. But if Johnny Wilde was even a little bit what he was supposed to be, I wanted him on my side. I stood in front of him and addressed him loudly by name. He broke off his one-sided conversation and heaved a long-suffering sigh, as though my arrival was just another burden he was condemned to suffer.

'Oh, it's that time, is it? Hello, Gideon Sable! I know why you're here. You want to hurt Fredric Hammer. I'm in. I disapprove of that man for many good reasons, not least for locking away all the wonders of the world so he can gloat over them in private. It shouldn't be allowed.'

I wasn't surprised he knew so many things he shouldn't. That was just par for the course with Johnny Wilde. He smiled craftily and beckoned for me to lean in closer. He glanced furtively

around and lowered his voice, as though not wanting to be overheard by all the people who weren't there.

'And, of course, I do have my own reasons for wanting revenge
on Fredric Hammer. I should be beyond such small things, but
I take it as proof of how rational I actually am, that I'm not.'

He jumped to his feet and performed a brisk soft-shoe routine
on top of the headstone, beaming happily. And then he launched
himself into the air, leaping from one grave marker to the next,
dancing across the roofs of old stone crypts and mausoleums.
Making a great circle around me and laughing out loud for the
sheer joy of it. He stopped suddenly, as though he'd run out of
steam, and dropped down to stand before me. His feet hardly
made a sound on the gravel. He pulled up a chair that wasn't
there and sat down on it. The invisible seat supported his weight
quite happily, so that he seemed to be lounging in mid-air. He
reached out with his right hand, and it disappeared into nowhere,
as though he'd thrust it offstage, behind the world's scenery.
When he brought his hand back, it was holding a mug of steaming
hot tea. The mug bore the legend *World's Best Visionary.* He
sipped at his tea, blew out a mouthful of smoke and fixed me
with a thoughtful look.

'I approve of your crew, Gideon. Getting Annie Anybody
involved in something big will be wonderful for her. And bringing
in the Ghost is an excellent idea; it'll do him good to serve a
useful purpose for once. I'm not so sure about the Damned . . .
He's always going to be more concerned with his own problems
than anyone else's.'

I was surprised and not a little impressed by this sudden attack
of lucidity, but I tried not to let it show.

'They all have something useful to contribute,' I said steadily.
'You can leave the Damned to me.'

'Gladly,' said Johnny.

A phone rang. Johnny picked up a handful of nothing and held
it to his ear. The ringing stopped. He listened for a while and
then put the nothing down again. He smiled brightly.

'Wrong number.'

I was pretty sure he was just messing with me now. I couldn't
let Johnny get to me, or I'd lose control of the situation.

'We've never worked together before,' I said. 'If you're to be a part of my crew, I need to have some idea of what's going on in your head.'

'Good luck with that,' Johnny said wistfully. 'Better men than you have tried and failed. Including me.'

'How did you become like this?' I said. 'I've heard a number of stories, but I'm not sure I believe any of them.'

'Really?' said Johnny. He leaned forward in his chair that wasn't there, and looked genuinely interested. 'What kind of stories?'

I tactfully chose some of the less scandalous ones. 'Some say you tried to sell your soul but ended up selling your sanity. No one's quite sure what you got in return. Others say you're possessed by some wayward faerie spirit. And there are those who believe you're the last living avatar of Dionysus.'

'Oh, I like all of those!' said Johnny, bouncing up and down on his invisible chair like a small child delighted with a new idea. But then the smile left his face, and he shook his head regretfully. 'I'm afraid the truth is far less comfortable. But if you must know . . .' He threw his mug of tea over his shoulder, and it vanished in mid-air. 'Listen to me, Gideon Sable the Second, and I will tell you who I am and how I came to be. And then you can tell me whether you're any happier for knowing.'

He paused for a moment, as though hoping I might change my mind, and then began his story in a brisk and rather distracted tone, as though he was talking about somebody else.

'I used to be a very well-respected professor of organic chemistry, at a very well-respected university which now refuses to admit I was ever part of its staff. I was synthesizing a new drug that was supposed to be a cure for some of the more extreme forms of anxiety, but I became far more interested in the reactions I was getting from my test subjects. Some of the thoughts and insights they were coming up with were absolutely fascinating – as though they were seeing the world clearly for the very first time.

'I became convinced that a purer version of the drug would be powerful enough to blow the doors of perception right off their hinges and allow an unblinking view of what holds reality together. And I wasn't going to waste that on a bunch of first-year students only doing it for course credits. So, after I'd refined the drug sufficiently, I took the first proper dose myself.'

He sat quietly, staring at nothing, and when he finally spoke again, his voice was very quiet and very sad.

'I thrust aside the curtains of the world and looked behind them. And what I learned . . . broke my heart, as well as my mind. This world is nothing more than a joke, and the joke is on us. We're all just playing a game, for Something's amusement. But now that I understood the rules and all the cheat codes that break the rules, I can do whatever I want. And I do. Because it's all just a game . . .'

'What happened after the drug wore off?'

'It never did, completely. Once I'd learned to see the world as it really is, I couldn't stop. I did think about blinding myself, but I was pretty sure that wouldn't be enough . . .

'I was fired from the university. For telling people truths they didn't want to know. My family and friends wanted nothing to do with me. It didn't matter. I couldn't take my old life seriously any more. But then Fredric Hammer decided he wanted the drug – not to take himself, but for his collection. Unfortunately for him, I never wrote down the final details on how to prepare the pure version. So he sent some of his people to collect me. That didn't work out too well for them. But he keeps trying. Dogging my footsteps, interrupting my life when all I want is a little peace . . .'

He fixed me with a surprisingly steady gaze. 'It's time to bring the Hammer down. I would be happy to be a part of your crew, Gideon.'

I gave him Annie's new address and told him when to be there.

'I don't mix well with people any more,' he said sadly. 'Because I can see who they really are.'

'You have to promise me that you won't hurt any of my people,' I said.

'You have my word,' said Johnny. 'For what that's worth.'

ACT TWO
Planning the Heist

SEVEN

Telling the Crew What They Need to Know

But Not Everything, Just Yet

There are parts of London no one goes to by choice; they're just where you end up when you can't fall any further.

I was the first to arrive at Annie's little flat, tucked away in the back of one of those grubby old tower blocks that should have been pulled down long ago. People were never meant to live crowded together like battery hens. I hung around outside for a while, quietly checking that I hadn't been followed and that no one was paying undue attention to the tower block. When you're planning on going up against the worst man in the world, paranoia is your friend.

The inside looked even worse than the outside, which took some doing. The glass in the door had been smashed, and the deserted lobby had all the welcoming ambience of a punch in the face. There were unpleasant stains on the linoleum floor and angry graffiti on the walls. The air stank of spilled booze and stale piss. Some of the residents had been marking their territory. Annie Anybody had fallen a long way from who and what she used to be. Just as I had.

Except we didn't fall; we were pushed.

I had to walk up eleven flights of stairs to get to Annie's flat because the lifts weren't working. Although one look was all it had taken to convince me that I wouldn't have trusted them anyway. By the time I got to the right floor, I had spots floating in front of my eyes and I was struggling to keep my heart from jumping out of my chest. It is possible that I was a little out of shape, but you don't need a healthy mind in a healthy body to do the kind of work I do. Just a sneaky way of thinking and a hell of a lot of attitude.

At the top of the stairs, I took a moment to regain my composure and get my lungs working properly again. I was making a fair amount of noise, but no one came out to see what was happening. In places like this, it isn't only the cat that gets killed for its curiosity. I put on my best *Don't mess with me* look, just in case, and set off down the long gloomy corridor to Annie's flat. I had to walk carefully to avoid stepping in things. I finally came to a halt before Annie's door and checked to make sure I had the right number; this didn't strike me as the kind of neighbourhood that would welcome unexpected visitors. I couldn't see a bell, so I knocked politely. There was a long pause before a harsh voice on the other side of the door demanded to know who I was.

'It's the man of your dreams, Annie.'

The door opened just a little, and Annie glared at me over the heavy steel chain. 'I've been having some awful dreams these last few years. Thanks to you. Where are the others?'

'On their way,' I said. 'Now, will you please invite me in, before someone notices I can afford decent clothes and therefore don't belong in this neighbourhood.'

Annie sniffed, took off the chain and opened the door. I slipped past her, and she quickly closed the door behind me and put the chain back in place. We stood and looked at each other for a long moment. I almost didn't recognize her. Wrapped in a long robe that was only one step up from a blanket, Annie had bare feet, no makeup on, and her hair was a severe buzzcut. She looked as if she was auditioning to be homeless. When not arrayed in her full glamour attire, or immersed in a role, she almost wasn't there. She glowered at me, arms tightly folded, daring me to make any comment. I gave her my best winning smile.

'Don't,' she said immediately. 'Save that for the marks.'

'Sorry. Just trying to be friendly.'

'Save that for someone who gives a damn. This is business, not an excuse to put the old team back together.'

'It could be.'

Her gaze was cold and unflinching. 'You must know that's never going to happen. We're not good for each other.'

'We used to be.'

'And look where that got us.'

'Things will be different this time,' I said confidently.

She just shook her head, as though some things were simply too obvious to need saying.

'Do you want some tea?'

'If you've got the kettle on,' I said.

She shrugged indifferently. 'Make yourself at home, because you will anyway. I'd tell you not to steal anything, but it's not like there's anything here worth taking.'

She shuffled off into the adjoining kitchen, leaving me to look the place over. It broke my heart to see Annie living in such a shithole. Jagged cracks in the ceiling and patches of mould on the walls; third-hand furniture with long scratch marks and hardly any veneer; and a carpet so faded it was practically colourless. Dust and grime, and trash scattered across the floor – all the signs of someone who just didn't care any more.

I remembered our old place, back when we were still a winning team and living high on the hog, surrounded by the loot and luxuries from a hundred triumphant cons. Nothing was too good for us, as long as we took it from somebody else. We thought the good times would go on for ever, the two of us against the world . . . But we were young then, with no idea the world had such big teeth.

Most of the room was taken up with Annie's tools of the trade. Assorted wigs on Styrofoam heads, long racks of clothes in every conceivable style, and a makeup table with a brightly lit mirror. Everything Annie needed to be anyone at all. There were photos all over the place, standing in frames on the furniture or just tacked to the walls, every single one of them an example of Annie in her various guises. Each photo had a handwritten name tag, as though to remind her which identity went with which look. There were no photos of anybody else, and definitely not one of me.

Annie emerged from her tiny kitchen with two mugs of tea. Just cheap things – no cartoon artwork or funny sayings – as though Annie no longer had room in her life for frivolous things. She thrust one of the mugs at me, and I took a quick sip in self-defence.

'Two sugars,' I said. 'You remembered.'

'Don't make anything of it,' said Annie. 'It's just habit.'

She gestured at two battered armchairs with stuffing hanging out of them, set facing each other in front of a single-bar electric fire, and we sat down opposite each other. I looked around the flat, trying to think of something nice to say that wouldn't get me laughed out of court.

'It is awful, isn't it?' said Annie. 'But it's all I can afford. Thanks to you.'

'That's not fair,' I said.

'I ended up here because I trusted you!'

'Then trust me again,' I said steadily. 'To help you get back in the game, and out of here.'

She sighed, staring down into her tea. 'I'd just about got used to living like this, and then you had to turn up and give me hope again, you bastard. Why did you come back, Gideon?'

For you, I thought but didn't say.

'Because I need your talents, and your gift, for the heist,' I said.

'What about what I need?'

'You need a chance for revenge on Hammer,' I said. 'The man who's really responsible for all of this.'

'Maybe,' said Annie. 'But what makes you think you're the one who can take down Fredric Hammer?'

'I can do it, because I have a very special "Get out of jail free" card,' I said. 'Or, more properly, a "Get into Hammer's private vault and rob him blind" card.'

She looked at me, trying hard not to seem too interested. 'How did you get hold of something like that?'

I grinned. 'I stole it.'

'Of course you did.'

She almost smiled at me. I smiled at her anyway.

'So . . . How are you doing, Annie?'

'How do you think? I'm just . . . getting through my life, one day at a time.'

'Are you looking forward to the heist?'

She gave me a hard look. 'To risking my life, and everything I've got, on yet another of your over-confident schemes?'

I made a point of not looking round at her flat. 'Do you really have that much to lose?'

'It may not be much, but it's mine,' she said quietly. 'I've lost so much already that you wouldn't think I cared, but I do.'

'If we do this right, all your troubles will be over.'

'I've heard that from you before,' said Annie. 'And . . . it's been a long time since I did anything like this.'

'What have you been doing?'

She shrugged. 'Industrial espionage, honey traps, the occasional spot of escorting when times get hard.'

She studied my face intently, but I was careful to keep my expression entirely non-judgemental.

'You've been away for some time,' Annie said finally. 'I heard you got out and left all the weird stuff behind you. So what have *you* been doing?'

'Keeping my head down and biding my time. Living an ordinary life, in the ordinary world. But I could never forget who I used to be, or that I belonged here, with you.'

'Don't push your luck,' said Annie.

I had to grin. 'That's practically my job description. You have your gift, and I have mine. The gift of the gab.'

'But my gift isn't reliable any more.' She looked at her tea again, so she wouldn't have to look at me.

'It'll come back to you,' I said easily. 'I have faith in you.'

She smiled briefly. 'You always knew how to say the cruellest things. Why are you so determined to go after Hammer, Gideon? You of all people have good reason to know how dangerous that man can be.'

'He'll be a hard nut to crack,' I said, 'but we have professional-level sneakiness on our side. I've put a lot of thought and planning into this heist, Annie. It's our chance to win big and get our own back on Hammer. To be a team again, and the kind of people we used to believe we were.'

'Too much time has passed,' said Annie. 'I don't think I can be that person any more.'

'Come on; what happened to all the dreams we used to have?'

'They got turned into nightmares. Because we tried to fly too high, too close to the sun, and got burned.'

'But we had a hell of a view while we were up there.'

And then we both looked round sharply as we heard heavy footsteps approaching down the corridor. They didn't sound at all friendly. We were both up and out of our chairs in a moment. I shot a quick look at the locked and chained door. It didn't look as if it could keep out anyone determined to get in.

'Whoever that is,' I said quietly, 'they don't seem to care that we know they're coming.'

'It's not one of ours?'

'I wouldn't have expected one of the others to get here this early.'

'Could Hammer have found out about us already?' Annie said suddenly.

'No,' I said. 'That's not possible . . .'

'This is Fredric Hammer we're talking about! He has people everywhere! Gideon, are you carrying?'

'You mean a weapon? You know I never use them.'

'People change.'

'I'll never change that much.'

'You might have to if we're going up against Hammer.'

The footsteps finally came to a halt, right outside the door. Without realizing, Annie moved a little closer to me. There was a long pause. Not a sound from out in the corridor.

'Why haven't they knocked?' Annie said quietly.

'Maybe they're looking for the bell.'

'There isn't one.'

'That would explain it.' I looked quickly around the flat. 'Not that I'm saying we need one, but . . . is there another way out of here?'

'Just the window,' said Annie. 'Which isn't particularly useful, unless you've got a rope ladder or a parachute under your jacket.'

'Of course not,' I said. 'That would ruin the style.'

We both stared at the door. It was worryingly quiet out in the corridor.

'Maybe you shouldn't have got rid of that lucky charm after all,' said Annie.

The door slammed open, snapping the steel chain, and the Damned strode in. He elbowed the door shut again without looking round and studied us both coldly. He was wearing a dark suit that fitted where it touched, like a predator wearing the skin of one of its kills. I thought the Damned looked a little less impressive for being seen in daylight . . . but even so, just standing there, his presence filled the flat. He seemed too big for the world, as though he might break anything he touched.

'Annie,' I said, in my steadiest voice, 'allow me to present Lex Talon, known for very good reason as the Damned. Lex, this is Annie Anybody. Please be nice.'

He nodded stiffly to Annie. 'Charmed.'

Annie just glared right back at him. 'Don't you ever knock?'

'I don't believe in giving warnings,' said Lex. He turned his unrelenting gaze on me. 'Where are the others?'

'They'll be here,' I said, doing my best to sound entirely convinced about that.

'I'd better check the door is secure,' said Annie. She glared at Lex. 'And if there's any damage, you can pay to put it right.'

She walked right at Lex, and he stepped out of her way at the very last moment. I was quietly pleased that Annie hadn't lost her nerve, and that Lex was ready to at least have a go at being civilized. I gave him my best hard look anyway.

'Why were you hanging around outside for so long?'

'It's been a long time since I was part of the world,' Lex said slowly. 'I was trying to remember how people behave.'

'Well,' I said, 'you almost got it right.'

Annie hadn't even reached the door when it suddenly burst open again and the Wild Card came bouncing in. He went charging round the flat, talking a mile a minute and taking a keen interest in everything, before finally crashing to a halt in front of us, beaming all over his face.

'Hello! Hello! Good to be here, good to be anywhere really, given the alternative. I know you, don't I . . . Yes! Gideon Sable, or very nearly. And you must be Annie Anybody, because I can't see the large glowering person here getting into any of those dresses. Which means you must be the Damned! I thought you'd be scarier.'

'I am,' said Lex.

Johnny Wilde smiled vaguely at all of us, as though already having trouble remembering our names or why he was there. He grabbed my mug of tea, took a good mouthful and spat it out. He tossed the mug over his shoulder and it vanished in mid-air. Johnny's arms were suddenly full of a large bunch of brightly coloured flowers, which he presented to Annie with a courteous bow.

'For you, my dear. To celebrate our first meeting, I bring living things cut down in their prime. I'm a great believer in tradition. And it's not like there's ever any shortage of flowers in a cemetery, which is where I happen to be residing at the moment, because it's peaceful and I can hear myself not thinking.'

He pushed the flowers into Annie's hands, and she did her best to look pleased.

'They smell lovely,' said Annie. 'I'd better put them in some water . . .'

'If you think it'll do any good,' Johnny said doubtfully. 'But you're only giving them false hope.'

He spun suddenly round to stare intently at Lex, not even slightly impressed by the man's presence.

'Hello there, big boy! Are those halos on your wrists or are you just pleased to see me? The voices tell me that you're damned, but what the hell – it happens to all the best people. I know a funny story about Heaven and Hell, which is all the funnier for being true. Remind me not to tell it to you later if you like sleeping . . . Ooh! Look at that!'

And he went bouncing off round the room again, peering closely at everything in case it might be faking, and still chattering happily away, not in the least bothered by our lack of response.

'Love what you haven't done with the place, Annie. It's so all of you. With this many different identities crammed together in one room, it's like being stuck in the middle of a party where everyone is shouting at once. Like the ghosts of everyone you've ever been.'

There was an almost desperate edge to his voice, as though he was trying to distract himself from what was going on inside his head. He snatched up one of Annie's wigs and tried it on, contemplating himself in a mirror on the wall that I would have sworn hadn't been there a moment before. He waved at his reflection, but the reflection didn't wave back, just shook its head resignedly. Johnny pouted sulkily, ripped the wig off and started to eat it. And then he suddenly seemed to remember that he wasn't alone, dropped the wig and turned back to smile bashfully at us.

'I'm not used to being among people any more. They break

so easily if I'm not careful about what I say. And it is hard to remember my people skills when there's so little left of the person I used to be.' He surprised me then with a perfectly sane smile. 'But there's a lot of that going around, isn't there?'

'Take it easy, Johnny,' I said. 'You're among friends. You don't need to impress anyone with how weird you are.'

'Thank you for bringing me on to this team, Gideon,' he said, his voice still hanging on to normality by its fingernails. 'I do like to keep busy, and I really am looking forward to making Fredric Hammer cry like a baby.'

He thrust out a hand for me to shake. He was standing on the other side of the room when he did it, but I could still feel a very solid hand grasping mine. I shook it solemnly, and the hand crumpled like paper and faded away.

'I'll just put these flowers in a vase,' said Annie.

'What flowers?' said Johnny.

Annie looked down and found her arms were empty. The bouquet had disappeared while we were all concentrating on other things. Annie glared at Johnny, who seemed honestly puzzled as to why she was so upset. He shrugged quickly and rushed over to plant himself right in front of Lex again. He stared intently into Lex's face, as though searching for something, and the Damned growled at him warningly.

'Down, boy!' said Johnny.

A dog biscuit appeared in his hand out of nowhere, and as Lex opened his mouth to say something, Johnny popped the biscuit in. Lex started to spit it out and then decided he liked it. He crunched the biscuit noisily, while Johnny looked at him proudly, as though he'd just taught an old dog a new trick. And who was to say he hadn't?

Annie shot me a look that said very clearly, *This is all your fault . . .*

'Isn't this nice?' I said brightly. 'And I was worried you wouldn't get on together . . .'

'I can get on with anyone,' Johnny said frostily. 'It's other people who have problems getting on with me. It's not my fault I'm complicated . . .'

Lex swallowed the last of his biscuit and looked at him thoughtfully. 'You're not scared of me. That's unusual.'

'There's nothing in this world that can scare me any more,' said Johnny, just a bit sadly.

'You do know I could crush you with my thumb?' said Lex.

'I'd only bounce back,' said Johnny. 'The material world no longer has jurisdiction over me, because I have supernatural immunity. Cause and consequence just slip and slide around me like water off a duck's back. Now, that is interesting . . . Normally, when I tell people things like that, they have the good sense to be very disturbed, but you're not even a little bit scared of me, are you, Lex? Even though you see me more clearly than most, because those awful things on your wrist mean you have a foot in other worlds. You don't just wear those halos; they wear you.'

'Do you know how to give them back?' said Lex.

'Why would you want to?' Johnny shrugged easily. 'If you could only see what I've seen, you wouldn't be nearly so concerned about the Hereafter. You might be a lot more worried about other things, but . . . You look so alone, my dear fellow. Is there anything I can do for you?'

Lex smiled. 'Do you have another biscuit?'

'Um . . . hello?'

None of us had realized the Ghost was there with us until he announced his presence in a quietly deferential voice. We all jumped a little, even Lex, though he tried very hard to look as if he hadn't. The Ghost was difficult to make out at first – little more than a human shape formed out of smoke – but under the pressure of so many gazes, he abruptly snapped into sharp focus, as though he needed everyone's attention before he could be sure he really was there.

The Ghost was standing in the furthest corner of the room, although hovering would probably have been a better term, given that his feet didn't quite reach the floor. It was always possible he'd forgotten they were supposed to. His clothes were a little more detailed than the last time I'd seen him, even if the colours were all over the place, suggesting he was making a special effort. And his long, white hair still drifted slowly this way and that, stirred by some unnatural breeze.

'How long have you been there?' said Annie.

The Ghost frowned thoughtfully. 'That's a time question, isn't it? I've never been very good with time . . .'

'Have you been listening to us?' said Annie.

'Who can say?'

'At least you're in the right place,' I said quickly. 'Did you have any trouble finding your way here?'

'Of course not; I just used my spiritual sat nav.' His solemn face gave way to a sudden grin as he took in the look on our faces. 'The things you people will believe . . . Look, I know London. I've spent most of my death walking up and down in it, getting to know its streets and its secrets. It helps keep me focused. I'm not trapped in Soho; it's just the nearest thing to a home I have. My preferred haunting ground. I have to say, though, I am pleased, and not a little surprised, that you can all see and hear me.'

'My halos allow me to see anything that might pose a threat,' said Lex.

'And I stole more than one gift, back in the day,' said Annie.

I had to raise an eyebrow at that. 'You've been holding out on me.'

'You haven't been a part of my life for years,' she said coldly. 'I don't have to tell you everything any more.'

I let that pass for the moment and smiled around the group.

'Annie Anybody, the Damned, the Wild Card and the Ghost – myths and legends of old London town, brought together to do something none of you could hope to do alone. I take it you have all at least heard of each other?'

There was a general nodding of heads. Reputations are currency in our line of work.

'But none of you have ever met before, let alone worked the same job together,' I said. 'Which is at least partly why I chose you. Hammer doesn't have the imagination to anticipate a crew like this, so he'll never see us coming.'

Lex looked at Annie. 'Is he always this upbeat?'

'Yes,' said Annie. 'Dreadful, isn't it?'

Lex shrugged. 'Makes a change.'

'Right, then! I think we've enjoyed as much small talk as we can stand,' I said brightly. 'Let us move on to more important matters.'

Annie and I sat down in the two uncomfortable armchairs. She pulled hers into position beside mine without thinking, as

though we were still partners in crime. I hid a smile and didn't
say anything.

'I'm sorry there aren't any more chairs,' said Annie. 'I'm not
used to having visitors.'

'Should I get some more from the next room?' I said.

'There aren't any more,' said Annie, not looking at me.

'Not to worry,' said the Ghost. He lifted his feet a little higher
and hovered happily in mid-air. Johnny sat down on an invisible
seat, which, from his motions, was now apparently a rocking
chair. Lex just folded his arms and leaned against the nearest
wall. All of them looked expectantly at me, and I smiled easily
back. (Act as if you know what you're doing, and people will
assume that you do.) I was still having trouble believing I'd got
everyone I needed for my crew, even if some of them were clearly
going to take more careful handling than others. I didn't let that
worry me; the best way to stay in charge is to be the man who
knows things.

'It's time to talk about the heist,' I said.

'We've waited long enough,' said Annie. 'No more fine words
and pleasantries; we need to know the details.'

'Then you shall have them,' I said grandly. 'Not all that long
ago, a well-respected Vatican priest and historian announced to
a somewhat startled world media that he had created a special
television that could show scenes from anywhen in the past. The
whole of human history was now available for viewing, just as
it happened. He promised that the very next day he would provide
a demonstration of his time television, for all the media who
cared to show up, showing actual scenes from the life of Jesus
Christ.

'Quite a few media representatives turned up the next day, if
only out of curiosity, but there was no sign of the device or its
priestly inventor. Instead, a stern-faced Vatican spokesman
announced that the viewing had been postponed – indefinitely.
The priest had been very firmly retired and sent into strict seclu-
sion. The general feeling among the world's media was that the
priest had suffered some kind of mental breakdown and the marvellous time television had never actually existed.

'But it did. The powers-that-be in the Vatican had decided that
unrestricted access to the life of Christ was simply too dangerous

to be shared with the masses. The Church was in the business of faith, not history. So they locked the television away in the Vatican's Vault of Forbidden Things (I'm told it sounds more impressive in the original Latin) while they decided what to do about it. But before they could make up their minds, or be tempted into running a few test viewings for themselves, the television was stolen from the Vault by the original Gideon Sable. Who always said there was nowhere he couldn't break into.'

'How do you know all this?' said Lex.

'I'm getting to that,' I said. 'Sable didn't steal the television for himself; he sold it on, almost immediately, to Fredric Hammer. Because if it was weird and collectible, Hammer was always going to be interested. Given the supposed size of that man's hoard and all the incredible treasures he's accumulated down the years, I have to wonder if he heard the phrase "He who dies with the most toys wins" at a very impressionable age, and took it to heart. The time television is currently locked away in Hammer's high-security vault, set directly underneath his secret and very heavily guarded museum.

'We are going to break in, steal the time television and then get the hell out before anyone discovers we were involved.'

'So . . .' said Annie. 'We're going to sneak past all of Fredric Hammer's famously nasty defences and protections, break into what is almost certainly the most secure treasure house in the world, grab one particular item and then smuggle it out? All without being seen or caught – because if we are, Hammer will have every one of us killed in nasty and unpleasant ways. Have I missed anything?'

'No,' I said. 'That's pretty much it.'

'How the hell are we supposed to do any of that?' said Annie.

'What she said, only with even more emphasis,' said the Ghost.

'I have a plan,' I said.

'So you keep saying,' said Annie. 'But what is it?'

'I'm getting there,' I said cheerfully.

'I am pretty sure I have a blunt instrument lying around here somewhere,' said Annie. *'What is your plan?'*

'We have to take this step by step,' I said carefully. 'There are other things you need to know first.'

'All right, then,' said Annie. 'Let's start with who's putting up the funding for this very unlikely heist?'

'Hammer's ex-wife,' I said. 'The reclusive and only slightly barking mad Judi Rifkin.'

There was more general nodding. They'd all heard of the world's second-biggest collector of very valuable weird shit.

'She can be pretty dangerous in her own right,' said Annie. 'Or at least she has enough money to hire professional people to be dangerous on her behalf.'

'Judi has her own reasons to want Fredric Hammer hurt and humiliated,' I said. 'We can use that. She's already provided enough seed money to start the ball rolling, and she's ready to pay out big time, once we deliver the time television to her.'

'How big?' said Annie.

'Seriously big.'

'Keep talking.'

'Fredric and Judi did not divorce amicably,' I said. 'Apparently, there was a huge quarrel over which of them had acquired the best pieces for their collection. Words were said and accusations made – the kind that can never be taken back. After that, Hammer used all his money, influence and lawyers to make sure Judi got nothing of any real worth in the divorce settlement. They've been fierce competitors ever since – out-bidding each other at auctions, stealing items from under each other's noses, and spending fortunes on insider information to make sure they get to the good stuff first. I'm pretty sure Hammer is way ahead on points, because this isn't the first time Judi has been willing to fund a crew to break into his vault.'

'Why does she want the television, specifically?' said Lex. 'If half the rumours I've heard are true, there are all kinds of things in Hammer's collection that would be worth a hell of a lot more.'

'But the time television is Hammer's current pride and joy,' I said. 'Which is why having it stolen right from under his nose, and past his finest protections, will hurt him the most.'

'But why does he care so much about that out of all the amazing things he's got?' said Johnny.

I think we were all a little startled to hear such a rational question from the Wild Card.

'I'm not entirely sure,' I said. 'Perhaps he's using it to study history, to help him discover the present location of lost treasures.'

'Maybe that's why Judi wants it,' said Annie. 'So she can get back in the game.'

'Could be,' I said. 'Only Judi knows, and she isn't saying. All that matters is, she wants the television and she's willing to pay us very good money to go and get it for her.'

'Why did she choose you?' said the Ghost, just to show he was paying attention.

I grinned. 'Because she believes I'm the original Gideon Sable.'

'Doesn't she think you're a bit young for a master thief with a reputation going back decades?' said Lex.

'I just told her I stole a new face.'

'I had some dealings with Judi, back when I was still warm and breathing,' said the Ghost, just a bit unexpectedly. 'This was before she married Hammer. A bright young thing, with lots of money and not nearly as good an eye for art as she liked to believe. I sold her several famous paintings, which she probably still thinks are the real thing. I can say that, because I saw what she did to people she caught cheating her. You be careful, Gideon. She might not be as bad as Hammer, because nobody is, but Judi can still be pretty vindictive when she feels like it.'

'Leave Judi to me,' I said. 'I can handle her.'

'How are we going to find Hammer's secret museum?' said Lex. 'No one knows where it is. That's the point.'

'Ah . . .' I said. 'Gather closer, my children, because this is where we get to the good stuff.'

I explained about tracking down the original Gideon Sable's safe deposit box and what I found inside it. I demonstrated the ballpoint pen by stopping Time just long enough to slap wigs on everyone's heads. Apart from the Ghost, of course. Then I moved to the other side of the room and restarted Time. They all seemed very impressed. Though Lex couldn't take his wig off fast enough. And Annie made a point of restoring each wig to its proper mount, while scowling at me darkly.

I showed them the skeleton key that could unlock absolutely anything, and the compass I got from Old Harry that would always point to what I needed. Finally, I produced a small leather-bound volume.

'This is Sable's personal journal. Packed full of useful details about the time television, and why he sold it to Hammer in the first place. He discovered it could be made to show scenes from the future as well as the past, and so he used it to see where the television was going to be, on its way to Hammer's vault, and finally inside it.'

'So he could work out how to get past all the defences and inside Hammer's vault!' said Annie.

'Exactly,' I said. 'He could use the television as a Trojan Horse, to get all the advance information he needed to plunder Hammer's vault.'

'It's like having our own man inside Hammer's organization,' said Annie. 'Telling us all his secrets. To hell with Judi Rifkin! I say we steal the television and keep it for ourselves. Just think what we could do with it!'

'We can't,' I said sternly. 'Because we couldn't hope to hang on to it. Word would be bound to get out, and then Hammer would send his most vicious people after us. And so would every other collector. The time television is the motherload – a collectible and a treasure that leads to other treasures and collectibles. They'd do absolutely anything to get their hands on something like that. No, it's much safer to sell the television to Judi, for a whole lot of money, and let her worry about how to hold on to it.'

'Why didn't the original Sable go through with his plan to loot Hammer's vault?' said the Ghost.

'I think he was still planning on how best to do that when he disappeared,' I said.

'Should we be concerned about what happened to him?' said Annie.

'No,' said Lex.

The rest of the crew looked at him, but it was clear none of them felt like questioning the Damned. He knew things. Everyone knew that.

'Where is Fredric Hammer, right now?' said Annie.

'Hiding from a world that hates him and wants him dead, inside his own secret museum,' I said. 'And no doubt gloating over his precious television.'

'Does the book say where this museum is?' said the Ghost.

'It tells us where to find the only access point,' I said. 'A carefully disguised dimensional door that can take us straight to the museum without having to cross the intervening distance.'

'Where is this door?' said Lex. 'Somewhere inside Hammer's old house?'

'No,' I said. 'That was one of the few things Judi did get in the divorce. Fredric's last insult to her: a big empty house that used to be full of all the wonderful things they acquired together. She's spent years trying to replace what she lost, and only managed to fill a few rooms. The door isn't there. Hammer knew she'd tear the place apart looking for it.'

'Then where is it?' said Lex.

'Inside a men's toilet, in a pizza place, on Oxford Street,' I said.

There was a pause.

'Why?' said the Ghost.

'Why not?' I said. 'Would you have looked there?'

'Hold it,' said Annie, just a bit dangerously. 'I have to go inside a men's toilet?'

'You've been in worse places,' I said.

'This is true,' said Annie.

'It's the perfect hiding place,' I said. 'People come and go all the time, and no one pays any attention. Which means we can do the same thing. Once we're in there, my skeleton key will open the dimensional door, and – just like that – we're in business.'

'But where exactly did Hammer build his secret museum?' said the Ghost.

'In a massive underground cavern,' I said. 'I can't give you the exact location, because Sable could only describe what he saw on the television screen. What matters is that Hammer's museum is right in the middle of a great open space that we will have to cross without being observed, past any number of protections and booby-traps. Then we have to break into the museum, work our way through the building undetected and finally down to the vault.'

'What makes you think we can do any of that?' said Lex.

'The wonders of supernatural lateral thinking,' I said. 'Of which I just happen to be a grand master. This is why I chose you people in particular, to make up my crew – because of your very special individual abilities.'

'What kind of defences and booby-traps are we talking about?' said Annie, frowning hard. 'Does the book provide details?'

'Of course,' I said. 'Though we'll have to be careful. There are pages missing from the book.'

'How did that happen?' said Annie.

'Deliberately torn out, apparently,' I said. 'I don't know why. But it tells us all we need to know. We can expect to encounter poltergeist attack dogs . . .'

'I knew there'd be dogs,' the Ghost said gloomily.

'After that, there will be golem guards,' I said. 'Followed by a whole load of shaped curses, buried in the cavern floor like landmines. And, of course, once we get inside the museum, we'll have to avoid being seen by any of the small army of heavily armed mercenaries that surround Hammer at all times.'

'I'm going off the whole idea,' said Annie.

'We can do this, people!' I said, glaring round the group and willing them to believe me. 'Between us, we have everything we need to deal with everything Hammer can put in our way.'

'What if you're wrong, and we can't?' Lex said bluntly.

'If it was going to be easy, I wouldn't need a crew,' I said. 'Just concentrate on what we stand to gain: a massive payout from Judi and revenge on Fredric Hammer.'

They thought about that, looking inward rather than at each other, and then one by one they all nodded slowly. I allowed myself to relax a little. I had them.

'Once we're inside the vault,' I said, 'and we've located the television, I'm sure we can also find the time to help ourselves to whatever interesting little items we might take a fancy to. Hammer will just assume they went to Judi as well. Think of it as a bonus.'

'I want the immortality drug,' said Lex.

'No, you don't,' Johnny said immediately.

We all turned to look at him. He'd been quiet for so long we'd almost forgotten he was there.

'What do you know that I don't?' said Lex.

'More than you can possibly imagine,' said Johnny. 'Which is why I no longer sleep.'

'I want any item powerful enough to put an end to my existence,' the Ghost said quietly. 'I just can't do this any more.'

'We'll find you something,' I said.

I glanced at Annie, but she said nothing about finding something to control her gift, so I didn't mention it either. The others didn't need to know that her gift might not always be entirely reliable.

Annie looked at me thoughtfully. 'What do you expect to get out of this?'

'Revenge on Hammer,' I said patiently. 'Along with big money from his ex, and as much of the good stuff as I can cram into my pockets.'

'I don't think so,' said Annie. 'I can't see you settling for just that. But what else is there? You must realize you can't have boasting rights. You can't talk about this, ever.'

'I know,' I said. 'You'll just have to trust me to keep quiet – as I trust all of you to keep quiet.'

'Honour among thieves?' said the Ghost. 'You sweet old-fashioned thing.'

'It's in all of our best interests,' I said.

'I think it's all going to be great fun!' said Johnny.

'That's because you're weird,' said Lex.

Johnny grinned at him. 'Lighten up, big boy. Or I'll set fire to your aura.'

'We need more details,' said Annie. 'Before we can decide whether this is actually doable. So, walk us through the plan, Gideon.'

'We all play our part,' I said. 'Johnny will persuade the security guards that we're not there.'

'I can do that!' Johnny said immediately. 'I can probably convince them that they're not there either, if you like.'

'The Ghost will spook the poltergeist attack dogs into running away,' I continued. 'And then manifest to any exterior guards and lead them on a merry chase, away from their assigned positions.'

'Why me?' said the Ghost.

'Because it doesn't matter if they shoot you,' I said. 'Once you've lured them far enough away, just disappear and join up with us again. By then, I'll have got us inside the museum with my skeleton key, where Annie will charm the security systems into not recognizing our presence.'

The Ghost frowned. 'But we're bound to bump into people as we move through the museum . . .'

'Not if we do this right,' I said. 'The book provides specific details as to where everyone will be, as seen on the television screen. From this, the original Sable was able to calculate a specific route that will allow us to move through the museum, unseen by anyone.'

'I could just kill everyone there,' said Lex. 'They all work for Hammer, so they must be guilty of something.'

'We're thieves,' I said. 'Not killers.'

'You said you needed me as muscle,' said Lex.

'To deal with any problems that might occur inside the vault,' I said. 'Some of the items in Hammer's collection have a reputation for being extremely dangerous.'

'They haven't met me,' said Lex.

'You're so positive,' Johnny said admiringly. 'It must be wonderful, being able to be sure of things.'

'We're going to need disguises,' Annie said firmly. 'All it takes is one person who's not where they're supposed to be – that Sable missed seeing on his screen – and just like that, we have a witness. We can't afford for anyone to see our faces.'

'I have my armour,' said Lex.

'I can be very vague,' said the Ghost.

'And no one sees me unless I want them to,' said Johnny.

'If we do this right, no one will know we were there,' I said.

'Things can always go wrong,' said Lex.

'I can put on one of my characters,' said Annie. 'So that just leaves you, Gideon.'

'All right!' I said. 'I will wear the burglar's traditional black domino mask. I've always wanted to.'

'Will you be carrying a bag marked "Swag", as well?' Johnny said hopefully.

'I think that might be pushing it a bit,' I said.

'Swag is an interesting word,' said the Ghost. 'Some say it was originally an acronym: stolen without a gun.'

'The things you know,' I said. 'Now, once we're outside the vault, you will walk through the door and confirm the television is still there. Annie will charm the vault's security systems into not seeing us, while I open the door with my skeleton key. We rush in, do the snatch and grab, and then get out the same way, only in reverse.'

'Easy-peasy, lemon squeezy,' said Johnny. 'What could possibly go wrong?'

Annie rounded on him. 'Never say that! It's unlucky.'

'Look around you,' said Johnny. 'Do you see any lucky people here?'

Annie turned away from him, so she could concentrate on me. 'What's our first step?'

'Hammer is holding a private auction, tomorrow afternoon,' I said. 'Selling off some minor items from his collection. Not because he needs the money, but so he can lord it over other collectors by showing off the amazing things he's willing to let go. I've already acquired an invitation, with a plus-one. That's you, Annie. The rest of you will have to get in on your own.'

The Ghost looked unhappy. 'Do I really need to be there? They say Hammer collects ghosts.'

'Why would he want them?' said Annie.

'I don't know,' said the Ghost. 'Perhaps so he can make them tell him things that the living couldn't.'

'What do ghosts know?' said Annie.

The Ghost smiled sadly. 'It's amazing what you can see when you don't have life to distract you.'

Lex and Johnny nodded in agreement.

'Which is why I need all of you to attend the auction,' I said, refusing to be weirded out.

'What if Hammer gets a good look at us?' said Lex.

'He won't be there,' I said confidently. 'Hammer hasn't left the security of his museum in ages. By attending this auction, we can get a sense of how his security operates, and how far he's prepared to go to protect what's his. And to see how the crew copes when facing Hammer's security. You'll just have to blend in.'

'What if his security people object to my presence?' said the Damned.

'We can always use Johnny as a distraction,' I said.

Johnny brightened up. 'I'd like that! I'm sure I could be very distracting if I just put my mind to it. It's been such a long time since I could be useful . . .'

'But before we visit the auction,' I said carefully, 'I have to pay a visit to Judi Rifkin.'

'Why?' Annie said immediately.

'Because she has insisted on a face-to-face meeting before we begin the heist,' I said.

'Then I'm going with you,' said Annie. 'To represent the crew.'

I raised an eyebrow. 'Don't you trust me?'

'Trust, but verify,' said the Ghost, just a bit unexpectedly.

'You've only just come back into my life, Gideon,' said Annie. 'I don't know this you.'

'Fine by me,' I said. 'We'll go see Judi together. But no one else. The less Judi knows about this crew, the better.'

No one had any reason to stick around once our business was done. The Damned and the Wild Card left together. Johnny had taken a liking to Lex, and even the Damned found it hard to say no to the Wild Card. They left the flat discussing low dives and lower people they had in common. The Ghost made a point of talking to me privately.

'I just wanted to thank you for bringing me into this crew. It's nice to have a sense of purpose again, and to feel a real connection to people.'

He started fading away even as he was talking, and by the end he was just a friendly whisper on the empty air. I turned to Annie, who looked at me steadily. There was a time I could interpret every thought that moved in her face, but all I could see now was a cold, impenetrable mask.

'I'll sort out a persona to meet Judi,' she said.

'Make it memorable,' I said. 'So she won't get even a glimpse of the real you. And I'll pick you up tomorrow. Whoever you are.'

EIGHT

The Woman Who Used to Have Everything

And Wants it Back

B right and early the next day, I pulled up outside Annie's tower block in my nice new car. She was already standing there waiting for me, but she didn't look like Annie any more. Her new persona was wearing an elegant gold lamé dress, elbow-length white gloves and a curly white wig. Pale-blue eyeshadow and white lipstick completed the new look: smart and glamorous and not at all dangerous. Not a bad combination for meeting someone like Judi Rifkin. I opened the door for her, and she settled herself comfortably beside me.

'You're right on time,' she said, her voice a good half an octave lower. 'I like that in a man. Call me Agatha.'

'Love the new look,' I said. 'But when we get to Judi's place, let me do all the talking.'

'Don't I always?' said Agatha.

'No,' I said.

'Then why would you think this is going to be any different?'

'I live in hope.'

'What is it you don't want me saying to her?'

'Any actual information about the crew or the plan,' I said. 'She doesn't need to know, and it will give her less to argue about.'

'You don't trust your own sponsor?'

'Please. This is Judi Rifkin we're talking about.'

'Of course. What was I thinking?'

I steered the car out into the heavy London traffic. It was a dark and brooding day, with oppressive gothic clouds filling the sky. Just the right mood and setting for meeting a famously rich and crazy lady in her place of power.

'Nice car,' said Agatha.

'I thought so.'

'You stole it, didn't you?'

'It would have been a crime not to,' I said. 'Someone had parked it across two disabled bays and didn't even have a sticker. So I embraced the cause of social justice and liberated this more than comfortable ride for a much nobler purpose.'

'You always could justify anything if you talked long enough.' She looked at me for a response, but I just concentrated on the road ahead. She tried another tack. 'So . . . what's she like? Is Hammer's ex-wife as crazy as everybody says?'

'People with her kind of money are never crazy. They're just eccentric.'

'But still sharp?'

'Oh, yes.'

'So for her, it's as much about the hate as the heist?'

'Doesn't make her any less shrewd as a businesswoman,' I said. 'A lot of con men have tried to take advantage of what they saw as her weak spot, and she had every single one of them served up for lunch. Judi may not be quite the monster her ex was and is, but she can do a pretty good imitation.'

'You can take the lead,' Agatha decided. 'That way, if it does all go wrong, I can always use you for cover.'

Judi Rifkin, ex-wife of Fredric Hammer, but still bound to him by ties of rage and loss, lived in a big old house on the edge of the city, and kept the rest of the world at bay with high stone walls and armed guards. The walls surrounding her property were thick enough to stop an oncoming tank and topped with iron spikes and rolls of barbed wire. There weren't any *Keep Out* signs, because she didn't need them. I pulled up well short of the main gates. I couldn't see any weapon systems, but I could feel the computer targeting kicking in. I lowered my window and spoke casually into the intercom.

'This is Gideon Sable. I'm expected. The lady with me is my allowed plus-one, so don't give me a hard time about her.'

There was a long pause, and then the intercom said, 'Stay in your car and wait for the guards.'

I could hear the whirring of the security cameras as they

changed position to get a better look at us. I sat very still and
kept my hands in plain sight, while doing my best to look as
though that was my idea. Agatha took her cue from me. After a
while, the crunch of boots on gravel announced the arrival of two
armed guards. They were both wearing flak jackets and carried
their automatic weapons as if they knew what they were doing.
So, of course, I just nodded to them easily as if they were merely
the hired help. Start as you mean to go on, or they won't respect
you in the morning. They took their time checking me out, without
opening the gates. One of them actually had a photo of me on
his phone.

'Judi takes her security very seriously,' said Agatha.

'I should hope so,' I said. 'There are a lot of thieves about.
And please, Agatha, no sticky fingers once we get in there. Judi
has absolutely no sense of humour when it comes to missing
property.'

'You have changed,' said Agatha.

'Keep your eyes on the big prize,' I said.

'Assuming we get that far,' said Agatha. 'Those guys have
very big guns.'

'Size isn't everything.'

The gates finally swung open and the two guards came striding
forward. They kept both of us covered with their weapons right
up to the point where they climbed into the back of the car.

'Follow the drive to the house,' said the older guard. 'No
detours, no stopping to enjoy the scenery, no questions.'

'What he said,' said the other guard.

'No sudden movements and no surprises.'

'Because we've seen it all before and weren't impressed then.'

'And keep to the speed limit.'

'Or we'll have to pull you over.'

'It never fails,' I said to Agatha. 'Put two guards together and
they think they're a double act.'

I eased the car between the open gates and was barely through
when they slammed viciously together behind us. The gravel
drive stretched away before me, disappearing into the distance.
It was all very quiet. The sounds of traffic couldn't get past the
high stone walls. The wide-open grounds were completely lacking
in vegetation. Presumably to make sure there was nothing any

intruder could use to conceal themselves. It was like driving on the surface of the moon. I finally brought the car to a halt right outside the front door of a huge, brooding mansion house. Built to impress and designed to intimidate, it wasn't so much a home as a fortress for someone who always felt under siege.

The guards got out of the car first and covered Agatha and me with their guns as we got out. I looked at the massive front door, which gave every indication of being strong enough to hold off an entire invading army, and gestured for the guards to lead the way. They gestured with their guns for me to take the lead, and I knew when I'd been out-gestured.

The front door opened on its own as we approached, and Agatha and I stepped through into a narrow hallway dominated by a great many security staff and a pair of heavy-duty electronic scanners. The kind they make you walk through at airports so everyone can see what you're made of.

'Please don't mess with any of the security equipment,' I murmured to Agatha. 'We need to keep your gift a secret.'

'I can't always control it, remember?'

'Try,' I said. 'Try really hard.'

I went through the scanner first, waited patiently while everyone and their friend took a good look at everything I had, and then moved on. The alarm bells remained silent, and I was quietly relieved that I'd decided not to bring any of my useful items with me. Previous experience had convinced me Judi would have her scanners set to search for anything that might pass as a weapon. I felt naked without my gadgets, and very much on the defensive – which was almost certainly the point. Agatha sailed through after me, holding her head high so she could look down on everyone. The alarms remained silent. The two guards looked disappointed, but they were philosophical about it. They moved in on either side of Agatha and me, and escorted us into the depths of the old house.

Everywhere I looked, the place was packed full of paintings and statues from all over the world – the plundered loot of past civilizations. Passing through the high-ceilinged corridors and wide-open rooms was like walking through a museum. Or the kind of stately home that never opens to visitors, because it doesn't need to. The paintings never got any more modern than the Pre-Raphaelites, and the statues were all defiantly classical (no fig leaves – everything on full display). I recognized enough to be sure the collection was worth several fortunes, but there was nothing that really impressed me.

Finally, we were ushered into an elegant drawing room of quite ordinary size and scale. The first human-sized setting we'd been in. Judi Rifkin was waiting for us, sitting on an ornate medieval throne, carefully elevated so she could look down on her visitors. Stiff-backed and steely-eyed, Judi was a well-preserved woman in her late seventies, with a pinched face, a wide slash of a mouth and short grey hair. Like the kind of grandmother you make excuses not to take the kids to see. She was wearing an extraordinarily elegant brocade gown and enough jewellery to start her own retail chain. As though she needed to make it clear to everyone just how rich she was, even though Hammer had left her. Agatha and I stood before her, because there weren't any other chairs. Judi gestured curtly to the two armed guards, and they quickly withdrew. I did my best not to tense up as I heard the door close and lock behind us. Judi leaned forward on her throne and glowered at me.

'This is your crew?'

'This is one of them. Her name is Agatha.'

Agatha dropped a surprisingly deep curtsy. 'You have so many wonderful things here, Ms Rifkin.'

'Feel free to look around,' said Judi. 'Take your time, my dear. Pleasure should never be rushed.'

She watched closely as we took in the paintings on her walls, and we were both careful to make all the right noises to show how impressed we were. The art consisted of erotic and even openly pornographic depictions of important people throughout history. Some of the scenes were indelicate, some were embarrassing, and a few were frankly disturbing.

'Magnificent,' I said finally, when I couldn't stand any more.

'I have so many wonderful things,' said Judi. 'And not just art. Do you see anything special here, Mr Sable?'

I turned away from the paintings to consider the various *objets trouvés* she had scattered around the room. Judi always liked to test my knowledge, to reassure herself I was what I seemed to be.

'The grand piano in the corner has keys fashioned from unicorn ivory,' I said. 'The wardrobe wrapped in heavy steel chains used to belong to C.S. Lewis. And I think I'm right in saying that this . . . is a Fabergé phoenix egg.' I went to pick it up, but the sheer heat radiating off the jewelled egg made me snatch my hand back. I smiled politely at Judi. 'May I compliment you on your impeccable good taste? You always did have a gift for acquiring the rare and unusual.'

'And I have money,' said Judi. 'Money buys resources, and useful people such as yourself, to get me the lovely things I must always have around me.'

To be honest, I still wasn't seeing anything worth getting excited about. There was nothing here that Hammer would have given house room to, and Judi must have known that. She sat back in her throne so she could fix me with her cold, grey gaze.

'You know your objective, and you know where it is. What is holding you back, Mr Sable?'

'My plan is dependent on very careful timing,' I said quietly, refusing to be intimidated. 'So that my crew can take advantage of certain in-built weaknesses in Hammer's security systems.'

'Ah, yes,' said Judi. 'Your crew . . .'

'You'll understand if I don't mention any names,' I said smoothly. 'I was only able to acquire their very special abilities by guaranteeing their anonymity.'

'And yet you brought this young lady with you,' said Judi.

'I can look after myself,' said Agatha.

'I'm sure you can, my dear,' said Judi. 'You have that look. What special gift do you bring to this criminal enterprise?'

Agatha smiled brightly. 'I distract people.'

'Of course you do,' said Judi.

'You hired me because of my reputation,' I said, bringing her attention back to me. 'My plans work, and I get things done.'

'Of course,' said Judi. 'But let security be your watchword, Mr Sable, when you go up against my ex-husband. He has spies everywhere. Even here, in my house, among my own people . . . I pay my people extremely well, but it's never enough. Money can buy security, but not loyalty.'

'He'll also know that you're the one who's taken possession of his precious time television,' I said.

'I want him to know! That's the point! Oh, you needn't worry; I won't breathe a word to anyone about how I got it. Because not knowing how he lost his favourite toy will do even more to drive him crazy!'

'Do you know why the television means so much to him?' I said.

'I don't know and I don't care!' Judi lost her poise for the first time, gripping the armrests of her throne so tightly her knuckles whitened. 'All that matters is that I will have it, and he won't.' She quickly regained control and settled herself more comfortably on her throne. 'I am an old woman now, Mr Sable. All I have left to warm my withered heart is the banked fires of revenge.'

'If you really want to hurt him,' I said carefully, 'we could always take an incendiary device into the vault with us and destroy his entire collection.'

Judi looked at me as though I was a barbarian. 'We are talking about unique, priceless items! That will one day be mine again. Your theft of the time television is only the beginning. I shall use that to prove to Fredric that there is nothing he has that I can't take from him.'

I looked at her thoughtfully. 'You're going to fund more heists, to steal more of his treasures?'

'Once you and your crew have established that it is possible to get past that man's defences, plunder his most secure vault – and get away with it. That will be all the proof people need that he can't protect his collection any longer. And then I shall have my choice of all the very best thieves to send against my dear ex-husband.'

'But what's to stop Hammer from sending his people here, to take it all back again?' said Agatha.

Judi smiled. 'Let him try. I have protections he has never even dreamed of.'

I just nodded. She wasn't interested in anyone else's opinion.

Judi sat up a little straighter in her throne. 'You must pardon me if I seem a little overwrought when it comes to my ex-husband. Even though he hasn't been a part of my life for years, Fredric is still the only man who can make my heart beat faster.'

'And you'll pardon me, I hope, if I ask you to confirm the payment details for the time television,' I said.

'Of course, Mr Sable. I haven't forgotten. Five million pounds, in cash, as requested.'

'One million for each of us,' I said, smiling at Agatha. She looked at me sharply but said nothing.

'Ah,' said Judi, smiling archly. 'From which I deduce there are three more people in your crew.'

'Your mathematics is impeccable,' I said.

'The money is already here,' said Judi, quite casually. 'Ready to be handed over, once the television has been delivered. And I shall expect to see the device demonstrated, to make sure it can do everything it's supposed to.'

'Fair enough,' I said.

'Which part of history would you want to watch?' said Agatha.

Judi looked a little taken aback, as though the thought had honestly never occurred to her.

'Perhaps I'll look into the future,' she said slowly. 'So I can watch Fredric die – alone, poor and broken. Or perhaps I'll look into the past, back to when Fredric and I were first married. And I was so happy, for a while.'

She rose from her throne and came down to join us, disdaining my offer of a helping hand. She limped stiffly across the room, leaving Agatha and me to follow on behind. I made sure we both maintained a respectful distance. I'd already spotted a number of hidden security cameras in the room. I was pretty sure that if either Agatha or I got too close to Judi, the doors would fly open and a small army of guards would come rushing in to slam us to the floor and sit on our heads.

Judi picked up a framed photo from an antique side table and stared at it for a long moment before showing it to me and Agatha. The image was of a much younger Judi and Fredric, smiling together. They looked to be in their twenties, arms wrapped around each other and very much in love. Two young and happy people, who had no idea of what the future held in store for them.

'I'm told he looks exactly the same these days,' said Judi. 'Thanks to his immortality drug. Not like me . . . But then he always was afraid of getting old.'

'The drug is real?' said Agatha. 'That's an actual thing?'

'Oh, yes,' said Judi. 'He drank it all, right in front of me – just to make it clear he wasn't going to let me have any. His last act of contempt before he walked out on me. Not for another woman – I think I could have understood that – but just because his precious things meant more to him than I ever could. Bastard.'

'So the drug really did make him immortal?' I said.

Judi shrugged and put the photo down again. 'It made him young . . . The Santa Clara Formulation came very highly recommended, with all kinds of provenances and guarantees from people who should have been in a position to know . . . But the only way to be sure is to keep watching him and see if he dies. And, of course, he is still entirely killable. Which is why he's always surrounded by his own private army.'

'But if he's so careful never to expose himself to danger,' Agatha said carefully, 'how can you hope to watch his death on the television?'

Judi smiled slowly. A very unpleasant smile. 'I have plans. Very special plans. I've spent a lot of time and money putting them in place. But then he's worth it. The only man who ever meant anything to me, who hurt me more than anyone else . . . So when I finally bring him down, I need him to hurt, too. That's why I never tried to have him killed. There isn't enough mercy left in me to allow him a quick death. First, I'll take away his collection, piece by piece. Then I'll take everything else he cares for. And finally, when he's just a poor broken thing . . . I might just let him go on like that. Living for ever, knowing I beat him.'

Her gaze turned inward as she savoured the thought. And then she seemed to realize she was revealing rather more of herself than she'd intended. She turned her back on the photo and stalked painfully back across the room to resume her place of pride on her throne. I could see how much that took out of her, but I knew better than to offer to help. She took her time settling herself and then smiled coldly down at Agatha and me, from perhaps the only place she still truly felt at home. A woman who had taken charge of her own private world. Agatha and I took up our positions before her again, and when Judi addressed us, her voice and manner were entirely businesslike.

'Understand me, Mr Sable. If you or any member of your crew are captured during your raid on Hammer's vault, don't look to me for a rescue or a ransom. If you reveal my involvement, I will deny everything. I'm not ready to fight an open war with Fredric. Not yet. Now . . . I think we've said everything that needs saying. I don't want to see or hear from you again until you're ready to deliver the time television. Go.'

I bowed politely, and after a moment Agatha did, too. We turned and headed quickly for the doors, although I did wonder whether we should be backing away, as one does with royalty. If only to make sure she didn't try to stab us in the back, just because she could. I did glance back, once, to see Judi sitting slumped on her throne, looking very old and very tired. Perhaps lost in thought of better times. The doors opened as Agatha and I approached them, and the two armed guards were waiting to escort us back through the house. Before we were allowed to leave, we had to pass through the electronic scanners again. The operators took their time, giving us a good look over.

'Is this necessary?' I said.

'Just checking to make sure something small and expensive didn't happen to jump into one of your pockets,' said the older guard.

'Please,' I said. 'We are professionals.'

'We know,' said the other guard. 'That's why we're doing this.'

Once again, they kept us covered with their guns from the back seat of my car, as I drove down the long gravel drive. The gates remained very firmly closed as we approached them, and I felt a faint flutter of unease as I wondered whether Judi had been quite as persuaded by my performance as I'd thought. But when I stopped before the gates, the guards just got out of the car and the gates swung back, and I had the car moving before they were fully open. Once we were safely through and out, I put my foot down hard and let Judi Rifkin's private world recede into the distance behind us. Agatha let out a long sigh of relief, pulled off her wig and scratched vigorously at her buzzcut.

'So that's Judi Rifkin,' said Annie. 'Surprisingly rational, I thought, for such a complete headcase.'

'And still very dangerous,' I said. 'She's buried a lot of people who thought they could put one over on her. Some of them were only napping. When it comes to planning revenge on her ex-husband, that woman is still sharp as a tack.'

'I see a problem ahead,' said Annie.

'Really?' I said. 'I see a whole bunch of problems. Which one did you have in mind?'

'You promised Lex the immortality drug,' said Annie. 'As payment for his taking part in the heist. But Judi seemed very convinced every last bit of it is gone. The Damned doesn't strike me as someone it would be safe to disappoint.'

'Just because Hammer drank some of the drug doesn't necessarily mean he drank all of it,' I said.

'But what if he did?'

I shrugged. 'There's bound to be something else in Hammer's vault the Damned will settle for.'

'You'd better be right about that,' said Annie. 'So, where do we go now?'

'Hammer's private auction starts in a couple of hours,' I said. 'I thought we might go somewhere nice for a spot of lunch.'

'Work first, lunch later,' said Annie. 'I need to go back to my place, so I can change into someone else. Agatha just wouldn't fit in at a top-rank auction house.'

'She did well back there,' I said. 'In fact, Judi seemed quite taken with her. I never heard her open up like that before.'

'I think Agatha and Judi would have a lot in common,' said Annie. 'Two women, both betrayed by their men.'

And she had nothing more to say all the way back into London.

NINE
Buyer Beware
And Watch Your Back

When Annie insisted she needed to change into someone more comfortable, I knew better than to argue. She always did find it easier to deal with a different situation by adopting a different persona. I parked the car on a double yellow line outside her tower block and escorted her into the lobby. There was still no one around, and it still smelled like the death of civilization.

'Where is everyone?' I said.

'Minding their own business,' said Annie. 'Be grateful.'

Back in her flat, she made me wait in the kitchen while she threw off her old identity and put together a new one, which only went to show just how long it had been since we were close. I killed some time by investigating the contents of her cupboards. You can learn a lot about people from their cupboards. The food was cheap and generic, but I didn't see any booze, which I decided to take as a positive sign. There was rather more dust and grime than I was comfortable seeing. People who don't care about the state of their surroundings have often stopped caring about themselves.

When Annie finally called me back in, she was wearing a low-cut dress in bright clashing colours, a flat dark wig, large round spectacles and far too much makeup. Plastic bangles clattered noisily at her wrists. She struck a pose and smiled at me sweetly.

'Hi, there! Call me Trixie. Just a sweet little bundle of no importance to anyone, whose outfit is always going to be more memorable than she is.'

I just nodded. I had to wonder if all these changes were Annie's way of hiding her real self from the world. So the world couldn't get to her and hurt her again. I also wondered if she felt the need to do this so often because I'd let her down so badly the last time we worked together.

Good thing I was around now to put things right. By endangering her life again.

'Let us away, to Hammer's auction,' I said brightly. 'And see how much trouble we can get into.'

'You haven't changed a bit,' said Trixie.

Someone had stolen the car by the time we came out, so we took the Tube across London, finally ending up outside a very well-known building in a very well-known area. The kind of place where you see more limousines than cars, and everyone knows your credit rating. Trixie pulled down her spectacles to study the situation and then raised a painted eyebrow at me.

'Isn't this . . .?'

'Well,' I said, 'yes and no. Yes, in that the building before us is normally home to the best-known auction house in London – but not today. Hammer has hired every last bit of it, because anything less would be beneath him. This very private auction will be held behind locked doors, and attendance is very definitely by invitation only.'

'And you have one,' said Trixie.

'Of course,' I said.

I produced it with a flourish: a heavy pasteboard card with elegant engraving and a built-in hologram to identify the owner.

'Let me guess,' said Trixie. 'You stole it.'

'Hardly,' I said. 'I couldn't risk the original owner reporting its loss to the auction staff. No, I bought this from Old Harry. Or at least I swapped it, for a child's doll from Old Salem that could speak in tongues. And yes, I did steal that.'

'All right,' said Trixie. 'How did Harry get his hands on an invitation to such an exclusive occasion?'

'It's never wise to ask Harry such questions,' I said carefully. 'He'll either lie or tell the truth, and I'm never sure which of the two I find the most disturbing. All that matters is that no one will challenge our right to be here.'

'What about Lex and Johnny and the Ghost?' said Trixie. 'How are they going to get in?'

I smiled. 'They have their ways.'

There were no guards on duty at the main door, just a single security camera peering down in judgement. Trixie and I marched up to the door as though we had every right to be there, and I held up my invitation so the camera could get a good look at it. There was only the slightest of pauses, and then the door swung open and we sauntered in.

A long empty hall led to another locked door and another security camera. I did the business with the card again, and we were finally allowed access to a massive open hall, packed with the rich and the powerful, the bright and the glamorous, wandering happily through the exhibits set out on display and chattering cheerfully. There were so many well-known faces that looking around felt like leafing through the pages of *Hello* magazine.

It seemed as much a social occasion as the preamble to a very private auction. Important people, out and about, so they could be seen being out and about. Uniformed waiters drifted through the crowd, offering drinks to familiar names from politics, industry and showbusiness, and other even less reputable trades. I availed myself of two flutes of champagne from a waiter passing by and handed one to Trixie. She looked down her nose at me.

'You know I don't drink when I'm in character.'

'Think of it as protective camouflage,' I said. 'Not drinking would stand out in a gathering like this. So, when in Rome . . .'

'Don't mention the decline and fall,' said Trixie. She took the merest sip, to show willing, and peered at the assembled throng over her spectacles. 'Do you see anyone else here from our side of the fence?'

'I wouldn't expect to,' I said. 'Even the most experienced grifter would have more sense than to try their luck against Fredric Hammer's security.'

'Then what makes you think we'll do any better?'

'We're gifted. And very highly motivated.'

Trixie just nodded. 'I have to say, I don't think much of the security so far. We weren't even body-scanned on the way in.'

'They scanned the card,' I said. 'Anything more would have been an insult to people like these.'

'You think Hammer cares about upsetting people?'

'Even the mighty Fredric Hammer has to acknowledge the social niceties,' I explained patiently, 'if he wants to attract the right kind of people to his auction.'

'You mean the high and mighty, who can afford the kind of things he's offering?'

'Not just that. Remember, this is all about Hammer impressing other collectors. He wants the right sort of people here so they can spread the word about what they saw, so all the other collectors will hear and be killingly jealous.'

'Who exactly are we supposed to be, if anybody asks?' said Trixie.

'We are international figures of mystery,' I said grandly. 'Let everyone wonder and beware. Shall we circulate?'

'Do we want to risk drawing attention to ourselves?'

'Not circulating would be far more likely to attract suspicious glances,' I said.

Trixie took my arm and smiled sweetly. 'Then, by all means, let us mingle.'

We strolled through the merry throng, nodding and smiling, and people smiled and nodded back because that's just what you did on occasions like this. But there were none of the usual hearty handshakes or air-kissing somewhere near cheeks, because once they entered an auction like this, they weren't friends or colleagues any more, just competitors. No one has any friends once the bidding starts. The only thing they had in common was their determination to not even glance at the dozens of security guards lining the walls, with their heavy body armour and automatic weapons. And very cold eyes.

'Are they here to protect the items set out for auction or the people who came here to bid on them?' Trixie said quietly.

'It's always possible that they're here to protect the people from the exhibits,' I said. 'Many of Hammer's possessions have a reputation for being extraordinarily dangerous.'

'Do the people here know that?'

'This is a Fredric Hammer auction,' I said patiently. 'Trust me: they know. On occasions like this, buyer beware comes as given.'

We wandered on, smiling relentlessly at one and all. Being constantly cheerful was surprisingly hard work.

'Maybe we should have stopped for lunch after all,' Trixie said finally. 'Do you suppose they do snacks here?'

'There are probably trays of the usual nibbles floating around somewhere,' I said. 'High on style and low on content.'

'Like most of the people here?'

'Play nicely, Trixie,' I said, still smiling determinedly. 'On any normal day, I'd be only too happy to rob these entitled parasites blind and leave them standing around in nothing but their socks, but we are here to work, not play.'

'You have mellowed,' said Trixie.

The exhibits being offered up for auction had been set out on separate spotlit plinths. Interested parties milled around them or clustered in small excited groups, like moths drawn to a flame. As far as I could see, it was all the usual stuff: rare books and objects of power, long-lost treasures and scary survivals from pre-history. Many of them with infamous names, sordid pasts and the kind of reputations guaranteed to make those in the know shiver, with fear or anticipation.

The Nightmare Church. The Abominable Childe. The Deplorable Lament.

They came in all shapes and sizes, including some that hurt your eyes if you looked at them too closely. There were no obvious protections in place, but still no one touched anything or even allowed themselves to get too close. Everyone present understood that the exhibits were more than capable of looking out for themselves.

'I think I'm actually impressed,' said Trixie. 'If these are the kind of things Hammer has decided he can do without, just think of all the incredible things he must still have locked away in his vault . . .'

'Hang on to that thought,' I said. 'Because in the not-too-distant future, we will be in a position to see for ourselves.'

And then I stopped before one particular item and frowned. Trixie moved in beside me.

'Problem?' she said quietly.

'According to the sign, this is supposed to be the Midas Ring,' I said, indicating the simple golden circle on a black velvet cushion. 'A ring that bestows the Midas touch, but with none of the traditional drawbacks. But it can't be.'

'Why not?'

'Because I was hired to steal the ring and melt it down, some time back. By certain vested interests who were concerned about what such a thing might do to the market value of gold. I watched the Midas Ring turn into a blob of molten metal.'

Trixie grinned. 'So not everything here is necessarily the real deal? I am shocked, I tell you, shocked. Are you going to make a complaint?'

'How could I?' I said. 'Gideon Sable doesn't know about it. Anyway, everyone invited to attend an auction like this knows the risks involved.'

Trixie glanced at the armed guards. 'Indeed.'

'Ah . . .' I said. 'I see trouble heading our way.'

'Why am I not surprised?' said Trixie. 'Do we stand our ground, run for the exit or throw things?'

'We smile and nod and make polite small talk,' I said sternly. 'And hope to hell the elegant bastard doesn't want to start something.'

The man heading purposefully in our direction was tall and distinguished, in his exquisitely tailored tuxedo, with a charming smile and cold, cold eyes.

'Where do you know him from?' murmured Trixie.

'All the wrong places,' I said. 'That is the renowned gentleman adventurer, Dominic Knight. And he knows the old me.'

'Did you work together?'

'We were briefly in competition over the same obscure object of desire. The owner wanted us to fight each other to the death for it, but instead we reached an amicable agreement. The kind where both parties can believe they came out on top.'

'What about the object of desire?'

'We decided we didn't want it any more.'

Dominic eased to a halt before us, struck an elegant pose and favoured me with his most charming smile.

'Hello, Dominic,' I said. 'What brings a cultured soul such as yourself to a snake pit like this?'

'The scent of danger and intrigue, as always. I might ask you the same question . . .'

'The name is Gideon Sable,' I said quickly.

He raised an elegant eyebrow. 'Really?' he murmured. 'I always thought he was a much older man.'

'I used to be,' I said.

'And how did such a notorious snapper-up of insufficiently guarded trifles as your good self manage to gain access to an exclusive gathering like this?'

'Because I was invited,' I said. 'My money being just as good as anybody else's. Or perhaps they just felt a need to test their security.'

We both glanced at the armed guards.

'I'm not entirely convinced their being here is in our best interests,' Dominic murmured. 'Or even our continued good health.'

'I shouldn't worry about it,' I said. 'It's not like there's any shortage of seriously overweight people here to hide behind if trouble should break out.'

He nodded slowly. 'I don't see any reason why it should, Gideon. I'm not here for you.'

'Then why are you here?' said Trixie.

His cold gaze barely flickered in her direction, before returning to me. 'I have my eye on something that I know for a fact isn't what the label says it is. I don't think Hammer knows exactly what he's letting go.'

'Hammer being wrong about something?' I said. 'How likely is that?'

Dominic just smiled briefly. 'I do hope we don't end up bidding against each other, Gideon. That could prove most unfortunate.'

He smiled at me, bowed briefly to Trixie and strolled away. A man of style and grace and occasional outbursts of extreme violence.

'Fancies himself, doesn't he?' said Trixie.

'Like you wouldn't believe,' I said.

Trixie scowled around her, at the crowd and the exhibits.

'I thought we were here to start some trouble?'

'I think it may well start without us,' I said.

I quietly drew Trixie's attention to the Damned and the Wild Card. Lex was standing stiff-backed in a corner, still inhabiting his ill-fitting suit, and glaring impartially at everyone. Even standing perfectly still, he looked more dangerous than all the armed guards put together. Everyone present was going out of their way to look in every direction but his.

Johnny was bobbing and bouncing through the crowd, taking a keen interest in everything, even when there wasn't actually anything there. Or at least nothing the rest of us could see. He chatted happily to everyone he encountered, and they smiled back at him with stark terror in their eyes until he moved on to bother someone else.

I looked around until I spotted one of the auction staff, resplendent in a long salmon-pink frock coat, with a stylized H emblazoned on his breast so everyone would know who he belonged to. I caught his eye and beckoned languorously, and he hurried over to see how he could be of service. I pointed out Lex and Johnny.

'How is it that such notorious characters have been allowed access to what I was assured would be a very exclusive occasion?'

'The Damned just walked in, sir,' the uniformed flunky said apologetically. 'And we let him, because no one wants to argue with the Damned. That doesn't tend to work out too well for people. So far, he seems content to keep himself to himself. We did send someone over to ask if he needed anything, and the Damned just stared at the man until he wet himself and ran away. So we are all now officially pretending that he's not there.'

'And the Wild Card?' said Trixie.

'He just appeared out of nowhere, madam, singing a very rude song by the Pogues and scattering rose petals, and then started stuffing his face with the vol-au-vents. We've had to send out for more. As long as he's not doing anything too upsetting, it's safer to just let him be. Hopefully, he'll get bored soon and move on somewhere else.'

'But if he should cause a disturbance?' I said.

'Rest assured that the guards are keeping a very close eye on him, sir.'

I had to raise an eyebrow. 'You think guns will work against the Wild Card?'

'These particular guns were supplied by Fredric Hammer, sir,' the flunky said carefully.

'And if they're powerful enough to cope with the exhibits
getting out of hand, you think they're nasty enough to deal with
every other kind of threat?'

The flunky smirked. 'I couldn't possibly comment, sir.'

'Why do you suppose the Damned and the Wild Card chose
to turn up here of all places?'

'Perhaps one of the exhibits caught their attention, sir,' said
the flunky. 'Or possibly they were attracted by Mr Hammer's
name. But really, sir, who knows why people like that do
anything?'

And then he had to excuse himself and hurry off, as the Wild
Card had started picking up some of the exhibits on display,
looking them over and putting them down again without any
obvious concern for how fragile they might be. A whole bunch
of flunkies gathered around him, at a safe distance, and tried to
talk each other into doing something. A few even looked to the
guards for help, but they didn't want to know. Johnny picked up
half a dozen exhibits and began juggling with them, while the
flunkies wrung their gloved hands and made polite noises of
distress.

'Shouldn't all kinds of alarms go off when he does that?' said
Trixie.

'Yes,' I said. 'But that's the Wild Card for you.'

Johnny lost interest in juggling, let the exhibits drop to the
floor and wandered off. While the flunkies were busy recovering
the fallen items and checking them for signs of damage, Johnny
took a sudden interest in a small carved wooden statue. He
picked it up, took a bite out of it and then put it down again.
Only now it appeared to be made of gold. Johnny moved on,
and the flunkies moved quickly in to study the exhibit. There
was a lot of excited murmuring, and then one of them picked
it up and carried it reverentially away. Several flunkies looked
thoughtfully after Johnny, apparently wondering whether his
presence might not be such a bad thing after all.

The Ghost arrived, walking through the far wall and several
guests who didn't even know he was there. He was wearing a
white tuxedo, complete in every detail, for reasons that presumably made sense to him. He came to a halt in the middle of the
room and peered about him, entirely unimpressed by the people

or the setting. When he turned his head to look at something, his long flyaway hair still took a moment to catch up. The Ghost wandered unhurriedly round the room, walking through people and exhibits in an absent-minded sort of way, as though none of them were real to him. Or at least not real enough to bother about.

I drew Trixie's attention to the Ghost. She winced and then looked curiously at the crowd.

'Are we the only ones who can see him?'

'Looks that way,' I said. 'And I'm guessing the security systems didn't anticipate having to deal with ghostly gatecrashers.'

Trixie turned her back on the Ghost and looked impatiently around her. 'How much longer before the auction starts? Only I think I've enjoyed about as much of the social ambience as I can stand.'

'Shouldn't be long now,' I said. 'The staff are just making sure everyone's had a good look at what's on offer.'

'I've never liked auctions,' said Trixie. 'All it takes is one cough in the wrong place and you can be the sudden proud owner of a real white elephant.'

'We're not here to bid for anything,' I said patiently. 'We're here to observe Hammer's security in action. Find out how far he's prepared to go to protect his property.'

'We already know that,' said Trixie. 'Look what he did to us.'

'But is he still relying on the old crude methods, or has he become more subtle and therefore more dangerous? We need to know. So we'll just wait for someone to start something, and see what happens.'

'This entire crowd looks depressingly well behaved,' said Trixie. 'What if none of them have the guts to act up?'

'Then *we'll* start something,' I said. 'Why do you think I told Lex and Johnny and the Ghost they had to be here?'

We sauntered back and forth, studying the various items on display with just the right amount of feigned indifference.

There were paintings produced by possessed children, depicting nightmare landscapes never seen by waking eyes. When the mind's defences fall away, in the deepest part of sleep, the unprotected mind can drift across all kinds of forbidden boundaries. Not every dreamer gets to come back from the places they visit.

A stuffed and mounted Sasquatch stood awkwardly in the middle of the room: eight feet tall, broad-shouldered and long-armed, with thick grey fur and a somewhat surprised look on his face. Up close, the fur still had a rank and feral odour.

'It's very well presented,' I said. 'I can't see a bullet hole anywhere.'

'Could this be the very last one?' said Trixie.

'Oh, no, there's a whole reservation of them in Yellowstone Park,' I said. 'This was probably just a rogue, caught out of its territory.'

'So they're not particularly rare, then?'

'Rare enough to provide boasting rights for whoever gets this,' I said. 'Probably stick it in the hall to impress their friends, or hang their coats on.'

A tall standing mirror contained no trace of our reflection. Instead, a scrawny wild-eyed man in rags and tatters hammered his fists against the other side of the glass. I waved a hand in front of his face, but he couldn't see it. He was screaming, silently and endlessly.

'Do you know him?' said Trixie.

'I recognize the type,' I said. 'He's one of us. Must have triggered some kind of trap and then found he couldn't get out. Hammer has always had a vindictive streak when it comes to dealing with those who have sinned against him.'

'How long do you suppose he's been in there?'

'Who knows how time moves in the mirror world?'

'Can you get him out?' said Trixie.

I looked at her. 'You think that's a good idea? He doesn't look in any mood to be grateful.'

'I don't like the idea of anyone being trapped like that,' said Trixie. 'I know how it feels.'

I studied the mirror carefully and even ran my hands surreptitiously over the wooden frame, before shaking my head. 'There's nothing here I'm familiar with. And since I don't have any of my toys with me . . . all we can do is walk away.'

'You're going to just leave him in there?'

'We can't help him. And I doubt this is the only upsetting thing we'll see. It's a Fredric Hammer auction, remember?'

As if to confirm that, the next item was a small pile of human knucklebones in a battered copper bowl, which apparently could be used to divine the future. The sign said the bones originally came from the living saint, Angelo Montini.

'I remember him,' said Trixie. 'He was all over the news a few years back. The man who could work miracles and did only good things wherever he went. Whatever happened to him?'

'He disappeared,' I said. 'No clues, no goodbye note . . . Nothing to explain why he just vanished between one planned appearance and the next. There was a real outcry for a while. Montini was very popular with the general public. The authorities set up a worldwide search but never found a trace of him anywhere. There were all kinds of sightings, like Elvis, but none of them ever came to anything. The current belief, in the more extreme religious circles, is that he was simply so good he was raptured directly up to Heaven.'

'And yet here are some of his bones,' said Trixie. 'What do *you* think happened to him?'

'I think Hammer happened to him.'

'You really think he'd kill a living saint?'

'Of course not. Hammer doesn't kill people. He has specialists to do that kind of thing for him.'

'But why would he want someone like Montini dead?' said Trixie, frowning at the knucklebones as though they could tell her something.

'It's not only bad people who have enemies,' I said.

Our next stop was before a small dark cube, maybe a foot on each side. It looked as if it had been carved out of a piece of the night sky, and staring at it for too long was like peering into an endless abyss. I had to tear my gaze away to keep from feeling as if I was falling into it.

'What the hell is that?' said Trixie. 'It's like staring into a hole in the world. Why isn't there any name, or at least a descriptive sign?'

'If you have to ask what this is, you shouldn't be bidding for it,' I said. 'You are looking at the infamous Box of Beyond. Supposedly, it fell off the back of another reality, which may or may not be there any more. It's supposed to contain the essence of entropy.'

'OK,' said Trixie. 'That sounds like a very bad idea and quite insanely dangerous. Why are we still standing here, instead of sprinting for the exit?'

'The Box could be quite appallingly dangerous,' I said, 'if anyone knew how to work it. Fortunately, it has no obvious control mechanisms. Although why any sane person would want to look for them . . .'

'Are you saying some people have?' said Trixie.

'There's always someone with more ambition than working brain cells,' I said. 'The Box is widely believed to be some kind of doomsday device, left over from an inter-dimensional war.'

'If it's that special, why is Hammer putting it up for auction?'

'Probably because he can't make it work,' I said. 'And he's hoping someone will buy it and work that out for him. Then he could take it back and . . . Actually, I don't know what could usefully come after that.'

'Gideon!' Trixie said urgently. 'That doesn't look right . . .'

The Box from Beyond was pulsing. Its sides surged in and out, as though it was breathing. And from out of its dark and starless depths, something was stirring and rising up. Something heading out of the night world and into ours. People around us were already backing away. Some called out desperately to the auction staff.

'I think it's time we retreated into the crowd and left this to someone who knows what they're doing,' I said.

'No!' said Trixie. 'You don't understand. This is down to me. It's my gift! The Box is waking up and trying to activate itself, just to please me.'

'Well, do something!' I said. 'Stop it!'

'I told you; I can't control my gift any more!'

'You have to shut the Box down,' I said, fighting to keep my voice steady. 'Because if that thing does activate, everything there is could just disappear. Concentrate! Tell the Box to turn itself off.'

'I'm trying . . .'

She stared fixedly into the darkness of the cube, sweat beading on her forehead as she struggled to win a fight only she could see or understand. I stood as close to her as I could, trying to support her with my presence, but I wasn't sure she even knew I was there. She was locked in battle with the Box from Beyond

. . . which suddenly gave up and went back to sleep again. Its sides grew still and the darkness no longer looked like a night sky from another universe. Trixie leaned heavily on my arm as I led her away. Uniformed staff quickly moved in, put the Box from Beyond in a reinforced container, sealed it and then carried it away. Very carefully. One of the staff turned to address the crowd.

'If I could have everyone's attention, please . . . There is nothing to be concerned about. Everything is under control. But I have been asked to announce that the Box from Beyond has been withdrawn from auction.'

There was a general murmur of approval and relief from all sides.

'Well,' said Trixie, pulling the remains of her composure around her again, 'we just started some trouble, and Hammer's security didn't do a damned thing.'

'I think we need something a little more obvious,' I said.

I looked across at the Damned. Still standing alone in his corner, and looking very much the poor relation in his shabby suit, Lex was glowering at everyone and everything with magnificent disdain. All the guests were being very careful to give him plenty of room, but there were a lot of surreptitious glances in his direction, and not a little animated conversation. It was actually something of a social triumph for people like these to have been in the same room as someone like him. Most people who met the Damned didn't survive to talk about it. Since he wasn't normally one for social gatherings, the general feeling seemed to be that Lex must have come looking for someone in particular. Everyone was watching everyone else for signs of guilt, if only so they could be sure of the right way to run when it all kicked off.

I caught Lex's eye and he immediately came striding out of his corner, plunging through the crowd and barely giving them enough time to get out of his way. They scattered before him like startled birds, making similar noises of panic and distress, followed by a certain amount of relieved laughter, once it became clear he wasn't interested in them. Lex finally came to a halt with his back to me and Trixie. He looked round the room, carefully paying us no attention at all.

'We need a distraction,' I said quietly. 'So people will forget the Box from Beyond only started activating after we got too close to it.'

Lex strode forward, picked a guest at random and punched him out. The man made a hole in the crowd as he went flying, and was unconscious before he hit the floor. Lex glared around.

'He had it coming!'

Everyone nodded quickly. A few applauded. The guards had trained all their guns on the Damned, but were apparently waiting for orders. The auction staff picked up the unconscious man and carried him away, Lex returned to his corner . . . and the guards slowly lowered their guns. The crowd burst into noisy chatter, interspersed with loud nervous laughter at having dodged some kind of bullet.

'Why didn't the guards do anything?' said Trixie.

'Probably because they didn't need to,' I said.

Trixie nodded slowly. 'Why are there so many of them?'

'To make it clear to everyone that no one messes with Fredric Hammer,' I said. 'Don't let them intimidate you; they're just thugs with guns. All you have to do is act rich and entitled and sneer at everybody, and the guards will assume you belong here.'

Trixie sniffed loudly. 'Like I needed you to tell me that.'

We moved off through the crowd again. The air was full of overlapping conversations as everyone tried to make themselves heard at once. They had a lot to talk about and were loving every minute of it. And all the while, Trixie and I walked unsuspected among them, like wolves let into the fold.

The Ghost came over to join us, walking through everyone in his way. Many of them shuddered briefly, as though they'd just heard someone digging their grave. The Ghost stopped before us and frowned unhappily.

'I'm sorry, but I don't see that I'm contributing anything useful by being here.'

I nodded slowly, apparently fascinated by the exhibit before me. 'I was hoping you might pick up something with your ghostly senses that we mere mortals might have overlooked.'

The Ghost peered dubiously about him. 'Some of the auras in this room are seriously disturbed – and I'm talking about exhibits as well as people. And not everything here is what it seems to be, but you don't need me to tell you that. I'm not seeing anything interesting or out of place . . . just the usual weird shit. And even if something should happen, it's not like I could do anything. Except wait for the trouble to finish and then try to comfort the suddenly deceased.'

'All right,' I said. 'You can go. We'll meet later at Annie's place, as agreed.'

'You're the boss,' said the Ghost. And then he disappeared before I could change my mind.

The crowd suddenly fell silent as two uniformed flunkies brought on a podium, so that a tall and distinguished figure in a morning suit could take up a self-important position behind it. He looked out over the expectant crowd and smiled briefly, as though he thought that was expected of him, before addressing them with cool indifference.

'Good afternoon. I am the auctioneer appointed by Mr Hammer to ensure that everything runs smoothly. Any time-wasters will be dealt with severely. Should there be any disagreements, my word is final because I speak for Mr Hammer.'

A frock-coated flunky brought forward the first exhibit, and just like that the auction was underway and we were off to the races. Item after item went under the gavel in swift succession, some of them going for seriously eye-watering sums, but there were no surprises and no real bidding wars. Everyone seemed to have a pretty good idea of what they were there for and how much they were prepared to pay.

This went on for a while, with everyone behaving themselves impeccably, until I decided I'd had enough and caught Johnny Wilde's eye. He brightened up immediately and came bustling through the crowd, grinning all over his face, talking loudly to people who weren't there and ignoring some of those who were. The crowd wisely chose to concentrate on the bidding and not do anything that might attract the Wild Card's attention. Johnny ended up standing beside me, looking in every direction except mine.

'It's time,' I said quietly. 'Make some trouble.'

'Love to,' said the Wild Card.

He walked right up to the nearest guard, snatched the automatic weapon out of his hands and fired the gun over the heads of the crowd. Everyone shrieked and ducked, and then tried to run in every direction at once. Johnny turned the gun this way and that, sending bullets flying everywhere. I grabbed Trixie, pulled her down on to the floor and covered her body with my own, silently cursing the Wild Card. He'd gone too far, as always. Johnny strode forward, giggling happily as he waved his gun around.

The whole crowd was panicking now. Screams filled the air. They kept trying to head for the exit, but somehow Johnny was always there to block their way. He kept up a steady stream of fire over everyone's heads, even though, technically speaking, he should have run out of ammunition long ago. If anyone had taken the time to look properly, they would have noticed Johnny was deliberately aiming so as not to hit anyone. But they were all too busy to notice.

Johnny darted back and forth, moving too quickly for any of the guards to get a clear shot at him, and he was always careful to stay inside the main body of the crowd, even as it tried to run away from him. But in the end, his aim wandered at just the wrong moment and one of the items on display exploded into a thousand pieces. And that was when the auctioneer stuck his head above his podium and gave the nod to the guards.

They aimed their weapons as one and opened fire on the crowd, shooting down the guests so they could get to the Wild Card. The roar of so much massed gunfire was painfully loud, almost enough to drown out the screams as men and women in expensive clothes were hit again and again. Their bodies were punched this way and that by the impact of the bullets, and their arms flailed wildly, as though reaching out for help that never came. Blood flew on the air as more and more people crashed to the floor. The wounded lay alongside the dead, trampled on blindly by the other guests as they ran madly back and forth, searching for safety and shelter that wasn't there. The guards kept firing, and the bodies kept dropping, and I huddled over Trixie and kept my head down.

Johnny realized what was happening and stopped firing. He threw his gun away and stuck his hands in the air, but the guards just kept on firing. Johnny ran through the rows of exhibits still on display, and the guards turned their guns to follow him, aiming carefully to avoid the exhibits, but not one bullet touched the Wild Card. The guests were still dying.

Dominic Knight cried out to the guards to stop, and when he saw that wasn't going to happen, he went to work, knocking the guards down while ducking and dodging their bullets with an ease that bordered on arrogance. He never saw the auctioneer draw his own gun, and probably never even heard the shot that took him down from behind.

He should have known this was no place for a gentleman adventurer.

The Damned was already tearing through the guards. Wrapped in his armour, he clubbed them down with his fists of light and darkness, and even the guards' superior firepower wasn't enough to stop him, but there were just so many of them. Some turned their guns away from Johnny to fire on the Damned as he bore down on them, but even the special guns Hammer had provided were no match for the Damned's armour.

Johnny ran straight at the tall standing mirror and dived into it as though it was a pool of water. The glass swallowed him up, and he was gone. The guards finally stopped firing and lowered their weapons, and a terrible silence filled the room.

There was smoke on the air, and blood and bodies all over the floor. Some of the dead were guests; others were auction staff. Some were guards the Damned had got to. In the sudden hush, the surviving guests huddled together, not wanting to draw any attention to themselves. Even the wounded did their best to stifle sobs and cries of pain. They might be rich and important people in their own right, but it had just been demonstrated to them that none of that meant anything to Fredric Hammer and his security people.

Buyer beware.

The guards were still covering the room with their weapons, even though Johnny was gone and the Damned had disappeared. Auction staff came rushing forward, ignoring the wounded and the traumatized to check how many of their precious exhibits had survived. The guests were on their own. They rose slowly to their feet, careful to make no sudden movements, but the guards just watched them indifferently. The wounded were helped to their feet and urged towards the exit. Some clearly shouldn't have been moved, but no one wanted to stay. The crowd headed for the door, and the guards let them go. No one looked back at the dead they left behind.

I helped Trixie to her feet, and she clung on to me as we joined the move to the door. We passed by the standing mirror the Wild Card had disappeared into. There was no sign of him in it, or of the wild-eyed man who'd been trapped there. The mirror showed no reflection at all. Two guards came forward and smashed the glass with their gun butts, and we moved quickly on.

'So now we know how far Hammer is prepared to go,' I said quietly.

'This was down to us,' Trixie said numbly. 'We're responsible for all of this.'

'No,' I said fiercely. 'This is all down to Hammer and the orders he gave his guards. Johnny went out of his way to make a lot of noise, without ever putting anyone in danger. The guards had to have realized that because they didn't do anything until one of the exhibits was destroyed. They didn't care about anything except protecting Fredric Hammer's property.'

Trixie nodded slowly and finally looked at me. 'You put your own body between me and a bullet. Risked your life, to protect mine.'

I shrugged quickly and kept her moving. 'Old habits die hard.'

'Thank you,' said Trixie. 'But don't get any ideas. Ours is still a strictly business relationship.'

'Of course,' I said.

We made our way down the long corridor to the front door and out of the auction house, leaving the death and destruction behind.

ACT THREE
The Heist Is On

TEN

To Make God Smile
Have a Plan

Trixie sat in silence on the Tube, all the way across London. She wouldn't even look at me. I stayed as close as she'd let me as I walked her back to her tower block, offering as much comfort as I could with my presence, and used the time to do some hard thinking. Given the sheer savagery of Hammer's response to such a minor disturbance, my confidence had taken a real battering, so I went to great pains to test my plan from every angle . . . but it still seemed sound. We could do this. And all the blood and slaughter I'd witnessed only made me more determined to bring Hammer down.

The moment Annie was back in her flat, she started tearing off Trixie's clothes and throwing them away, as though by removing the persona she could free herself of the bad memories that went with it. I didn't wait to be dismissed; the moment the clothes started coming off, I disappeared into the kitchen, where I used my knowledge of her cupboards to organize two big mugs of hot tea.

Time passed, but she didn't call for me to come back in. In the end, I knocked politely on the closed door, and when she still didn't say anything, I went back in anyway. Annie was sitting slumped in a chair, wrapped in a battered old dressing gown, all the makeup scrubbed off her face, staring at nothing. I pressed a mug of tea into her hand, and she took a sip without looking at me. I sat down opposite her.

'No sugar,' she said finally. 'You remembered.'

'Of course,' I said.

Annie slowly raised her head to look at me. She hadn't been crying, but she had the look of someone who'd been hit, and hit hard.

'So much blood . . . I can't say I liked any of those people, but they didn't deserve to die like that. They never stood a chance. Be honest, Gideon: did you have any idea something like that might happen?'

'Of course not,' I said. 'It was only supposed to be a fact-finding mission. Prod the auction's security with a stick to see how it would react. Hammer has changed since we last knew him. He always was ruthless, and vicious when it suited him, but what happened at that auction was way out of proportion. When I told Johnny to make some trouble, I was expecting invisible chains or a paralysis spell – some weird means of imposing control. I didn't expect men with guns and kill orders. Hammer had all those people butchered, just to protect things he didn't even want any more.'

'Well,' said Annie, 'at least now we can honestly say we know just how far Hammer is prepared to go. But you're still intending to go ahead with the heist, aren't you?'

'Yes,' I said. 'Because he deserves what's coming more than ever. Hammer needs to be hurt the way he hurts other people.'

'I'm not sure I want to be a part of this any more,' said Annie, staring into her mug. 'What's the point of revenge? Whether we win or whether we lose, we'll still be us, and he'll still be him.'

'Not if my plan works out,' I said.

'What plan?' She put her mug down and stared right at me for the first time. 'You keep going on about this amazing plan, but you still haven't explained anything about how we're going to make it work!'

'Wait till the others get here,' I said. 'And then all will be made clear.'

A door suddenly appeared in the far wall. A perfectly ordinary-looking door, except that I knew for a fact there was nothing on the other side of that wall apart from a very long drop. Annie and I were quickly on our feet and standing together, ready to present a unified front to whatever was coming. And then the door swung open and Johnny Wilde came striding through, looking very pleased with himself. He was followed by the Damned, who remained his usual dark and brooding self. Johnny started to say something, and then glanced back at the door and snapped his fingers. The door quietly disappeared, and the wall was just a wall again.

'I do like a conveyance that cleans up after itself,' Johnny said happily.

'I didn't know you had access to a dimensional door,' I said, with what I thought was considerable restraint.

'Lots of things you don't know about me,' Johnny said loftily. 'But one of the few good things about seeing this world so clearly is that I always know the best short cuts.'

'And it does beat standing around waiting for the Tube,' said Lex.

'Hold it,' said Annie. 'The scary and dangerous Damned gets around London on the Underground?'

'When I have to,' said Lex. 'You think a taxi is ever going to stop for someone who looks like me?'

'Don't you draw a lot of attention to yourself on the Tube?' said Annie.

'The halos ensure no one sees me unless I want them to,' said Lex.

'Must be a bit awkward on occasion,' I said. 'If someone thinks your seat is empty and tries to sit on your lap.'

'Trust me,' said the Damned. 'That never happens.'

I turned back to Johnny. 'How did you get your hands on a dimensional door?'

'Oh, they're all around if you know where to look. When you can go backstage like I do, behind the scenery of the world, you're free to help yourself to any of the props you fancy. But before you ask, Gideon – and given that gleam in your eye, I know you're going to – no, I can't find you a door that will take us straight to Hammer's museum. That man is seriously protected.'

'Even from someone like you?' said Annie.

'Especially from people like me,' said Johnny.

'I didn't know there were any people like you,' I said.

The Damned was suddenly standing right in front of me, glaring into my face. 'The auction was a bloodbath! The heist hasn't even begun, and already innocent people are dead. This isn't what I signed on for.'

I stood my ground and met his gaze calmly.

'First, there were no innocent people at that auction. Just knowing the kind of things that would be there, and wanting to own them, means all of those people had already crossed the line. And second, all those deaths are down to Fredric Hammer. We did nothing to justify such an extreme reaction.'

'We should have known,' growled the Damned. 'We knew Hammer.'

'He's always been a monster,' said Johnny.

'A monster who creates other monsters,' said Lex. 'Like us.'

'Still!' said Johnny. 'Life, death – what's the difference?'

We all looked at him.

'Are you being philosophical or just weird?' I said.

Johnny smiled sadly. 'Who can say?'

And then we all looked round sharply as there was a knock on the door.

'I am getting tired of unexpected callers,' said Annie. 'This was supposed to be the one place the world couldn't find me.'

'Could some of Hammer's people have followed you here?' said Lex.

'No,' I said immediately. 'I'd have noticed.'

'To be fair,' said Annie, 'he really would have.'

'Then who's out there?' said Lex.

'It can't be Hammer's people,' I said. 'Because they wouldn't bother to knock, would they? Open the door, Annie.'

She looked at me. 'Seriously?'

'How else are we going to find out who it is?' I said reasonably. 'Don't worry; you have all of us to protect you.'

'Lucky me,' said Annie.

She pulled the door open and there was no one there. She looked up and down the corridor, just to make sure, then stepped back and shut the door. The moment she did, the Ghost was standing there with us.

'Sorry I'm late,' he said. 'But that is my permanent condition after all.'

'Why did you knock?' said Lex.

The Ghost looked at him reproachfully. 'I was raised to be polite.'

'It's about time you got here,' I said. 'A lot happened after you left the auction.'

'I know,' said the Ghost. 'The street outside the auction house was packed with the spirits of the forcibly departed. It took me ages to get them all calmed down and pointed to where they needed to go.'

'Tadpoles and frogs,' Johnny said wisely. 'Caterpillars and butterflies. If we knew where we were going, we'd probably be too scared to go there. Different . . . is always going to be scary.'

'Shut up, Johnny,' the Ghost said kindly.

'All right!' I said loudly. 'Now we're all here, it's time to walk you through the plan.'

I took a map out of my pocket and then had to move several wigs on heads off a table so I could have a flat surface. Annie snatched the heads away from me, clutching them to her and murmuring words of comfort as she found a safe place for them. I carefully refrained from any comment as I unfolded the map and laid it out, and gestured for everyone to gather round the table.

'This is something I prepared earlier,' I said. 'Based on the information in the original Sable's journal.'

The crew studied the map carefully.

'It's a bit basic, isn't it?' said Annie.

'What the hell are we supposed to be looking at?' said Lex.

'Hammer hid his museum deep underground, remember?' I said patiently. 'This map shows the cavern floor surrounding the museum. You'll note that the museum is positioned right in the centre of the cavern, surrounded by acres and acres of nothing at all. So the security people can see anyone coming, from any direction.'

'What can you tell us about the museum itself?' said Lex.

'It's built like a fortress,' I said. 'Thick concrete walls, no windows and just the one door, made of reinforced steel. And on top of all that, a whole bunch of gun emplacements on the roof, covering the entire area.'

'So once we enter the cavern, there's nowhere for us to hide?' said Annie.

'A few stalagmites,' I said. 'Some rocks and rubble. But we shouldn't need them; you're going to charm the museum's surveillance systems into not seeing us.'

'Earlier on, you said the museum was defended by poltergeist attack dogs,' said Lex.

'That's right, you did,' said the Ghost. 'I've been worrying about that. I don't do well with dogs.'

'They're not actual dogs,' I said patiently. 'More like . . . invisible floating entities, with very big teeth. Living storms of psionic energies, given shape and form and a nasty disposition.'

'How does Hammer control them?' said Lex.

'I'm not sure that he does,' I said. 'More likely he just lets them run loose in the cavern, pre-programmed to attack anything that moves.'

'How many of them are there?' said the Ghost.

'Thirteen,' I said. 'I've marked the areas they patrol in red.'

'Those are big areas,' said the Ghost.

'If they're invisible,' said Annie, 'how will we know if they're heading our way?'

'We'll have no trouble detecting their presence,' I said. 'These are bad dogs.' I turned to the Ghost. 'Once they're close enough, you can just scare them off. Poltergeists spook easily.'

'Can I have that in writing?' said the Ghost.

'It's already in writing,' I said. 'It's in the book.'

'You also mentioned golem guards,' said Lex. 'I don't see them marked anywhere on the map.'

'Sable was very definite that they'd be there,' I said. 'But he didn't provide any locations or even a description. Maybe they just wander around.'

'If any of them get in our way, I will pound them into gravel,' said the Damned. And then he shot me a look. 'Or are you about to remind us again that we are thieves, not killers?'

'They're just golems,' I said. 'Pound away.'

'I'm more worried about the shaped curses buried in the cavern floor like landmines,' said Annie. 'What do they do, exactly?'

'The original Sable did some research on that,' I said carefully. 'Apparently, they can cause involuntary transformations and explosive combustion, and manifest sudden trapdoors that can send you plummeting out of reality. The usual.'

'Does the book say where they're buried?' said Annie, leaning over the map.

'Everywhere you see a cross,' I said. 'Lots of them, aren't there? Fortunately, they were laid down in regular patterns, with narrow paths left open for those in the know.'

'Can we trust these paths?' said Lex.

'We can trust the book,' I said. 'But this is Hammer, after all. So I thought we'd let you take the lead, in your armour, and if nothing happens, we'll just follow on behind in your footsteps.'

'What if there are some defences the original Sable couldn't describe because they never showed up on his television screen?' said Johnny.

It never ceased to surprise me when the Wild Card had one of his sane and rational moments.

'That's where you come in,' I said. 'Since the world has so much trouble seeing you clearly, we'll all stick close to you, and that should hide us from the bad things.'

'You're putting a lot of faith in me,' said Johnny. 'That's never wise. I'm not dependable, because the world isn't.'

'We can do this!' I said, staring forcefully round the table.

Surprisingly, Lex was the first to shake his head. 'There are too many unknowables, too many things that could go wrong. Hammer has always been very good when it comes to unpleasant surprises. We need more time to think this through.'

'We don't have any more time,' I said. 'All the information in Sable's journal is based on what he saw happening this evening. If we don't go tonight, we'll never get another chance like this.'

'Then perhaps we shouldn't go,' said Lex.

'You're the Damned!' I said. 'What have you got to be afraid of?'

'Nothing,' he said coldly. 'But I have armour; the rest of you don't. There will be other times, other chances, to get back at Hammer.'

'But he'll never be this vulnerable again,' I said. 'Of course there are problems and dangers, but with the book to guide us, the odds are stacked in our favour.' I looked around the table, meeting everyone's gaze in turn. 'We are in a position to do what no one else has ever been able to do. Kick Hammer where it will hurt the most, and get away with it, while making ourselves extraordinarily well-off in the process. Isn't that what all of us want?'

'Yes,' said the Ghost. 'Yes, it is.'

The rest of the crew nodded slowly, and one by one they turned their attention back to the map.

'This just shows the exterior defences,' said Lex. 'Once we get inside the museum, there are bound to be others.'

'The journal says not, because of all the permanent staff,' I said. 'All we have to do is follow the route the original Sable worked out, moving quietly from one empty room and corridor to another, and no one will have any idea we're there.'

'What if there are interior defences that only make themselves known once they've been triggered?' Johnny said craftily. 'Sable wouldn't know about them, would he?'

'Look,' I said. 'If this was easy, everyone would be doing it.'

'Talk us through the plan,' said Lex.

'Annie will charm the security systems,' I said. 'Not shut them down – that would be noticed – but just persuade them to edit our images out of their live feed. The systems will bend over backwards to please Annie.'

'Really?' said Lex.

'It's a gift,' said Annie.

'Well, that's just weird,' said Johnny.

We all looked at him for a moment.

'With the security systems on our side, we can cross the cavern floor unnoticed,' I said. 'And once we've got past the defences, we can head straight for the front door.'

'Hold it,' said Lex. 'Why not the back door?'

'Because there isn't one,' I said. 'A single entrance point gives Hammer complete control over who gets into his museum.'

'What will I be wearing?' said Annie.

I looked at her. 'What?'

'What outfit do I wear?' said Annie. 'Who am I supposed to be?'

'It won't make any difference,' I said. 'The whole point is that no one is going to see us.'

'No plan survives contact with the enemy,' said Lex.

'We're not going to make any contact with the enemy,' I said. 'That's the whole point!'

Johnny grinned at Lex. 'Excitable, isn't he?'

I took a deep breath and steadied myself. 'As long as we follow

the planned route, moving quietly from one empty room to
another—'

'But what if something unexpected happens to force us off
the route?' said Annie. 'How many people are there in the
museum?'

'Sable doesn't provide a number,' I said. 'Basically, it's just
Hammer and his security people.'

'That's it!' said Annie. 'I can dress up as security and
vouch for us if we're challenged. What kind of uniform do they
wear?'

I held on to my patience with both hands, because I knew if
I started shouting, I was lost.

'You don't need a new persona for the heist. Just be
yourself.'

'I don't have an outfit for that,' said Annie.

All of the others were smiling now, enjoying the show.

'No one is going to see us,' I said flatly. 'That's what makes
this heist possible. So we follow the directions as laid down in
the book. Annie will keep the surveillance systems charmed, to
ensure the alarms stay quiet. When we get down to the vault
door, the Ghost will stick his head through to make sure the
television is still there, and I will then open the door with my
skeleton key. We go in, grab the television, along with anything
else that takes our fancy, and finally retrace our steps back
through the mansion and out into the cavern again.'

'Just how sure are you that can we trust this book?' Lex said
bluntly.

'I found it among the original Sable's effects, in a safe
deposit box no one else even knew existed,' I said. 'And the
information in the book has already passed every test I can
think of.'

'But if something should go wrong . . .' Lex said stubbornly.

'That's why you're with us,' I said. 'To deal forcibly with any
little problem that might arise.'

Everyone looked at the map, thinking hard.

'Any questions?' I said.

'Lots and lots,' said Annie. 'Starting with: what do we do if
the plan should go wrong? If things start happening that aren't
described in the book? Do we press on or retreat?'

I looked around the table. 'We'll never have another chance like this.'

'We press on,' said the Damned.

'Improvising wildly as we go,' said the Ghost.

'I can do that,' said the Wild Card.

ELEVEN

Sneaking Up on the Sleeping Dragon While Being Very Careful Not to Trip Over Anything

It was late in the evening, and Annie was waiting impatiently outside her tower block when I drew up before her in my nice new ride. I got out and gestured grandly at my latest venture into the car-owning business.

'Well, what do you think?'

'Very nice,' said Annie. 'Expensive and stylish and very you. Who did you steal this one from?'

'A politician,' I said. 'So he must have done something to deserve it. Think of this as not so much a car, more karma in action. Now, I have a question. Why are you dressed as Marilyn Monroe?'

Annie struck a pose, bending her knees slightly and pouting at me in the famous Marilyn manner. She was wearing the iconic white dress and a curly blonde wig, but it was all in the look. She smiled sweetly at me.

'I couldn't go just as myself; I would have felt too exposed. So I came up with this. I'm sure it will come in very useful.'

'All right,' I said. 'I just know I'm going to regret this, but I'll bite. How is looking like Marilyn Monroe going to come in useful, as we put our lives on the line to go up against the worst man in the world?'

'If we should happen to run into a guard, he'll be so surprised and dazzled to see me that he'll just stand there and stare. Giving the rest of you plenty of time to take him down. And later on, when Hammer asks him what happened, all he'll be able to say is "I met Marilyn Monroe!"'

'But the whole point of this heist is that we won't be meeting any guards,' I said. Not for the first time.

'We might,' Annie said firmly.

'I can't help feeling that there's more to the argument than that, but I don't have the energy to pursue it,' I said. 'I accept that the look might come in handy, but I am still not going to call you Marilyn. I've already had to call you by so many names that I can't remember who did what, so for the rest of this heist you are Annie. No matter who you look like.'

'You're getting old,' said Annie. 'I can remember a time when you could keep up with me.'

'I can remember when you wanted me to.'

Her face was suddenly cold, and she didn't look a bit like Marilyn any more. 'We were different people then. Don't get any ideas, Gideon. This is strictly business.'

I just nodded and looked up and down the empty street. 'Where are Lex, Johnny and the Ghost? I thought I'd made it clear how important it was for them to be here on time. We're going to have to run a very strict timetable to stay in synch with Sable's book.'

'We're right here, waiting for you,' said Johnny's voice from inside my car. I turned to look, and there were Lex and Johnny in the back seat. I had no idea how they got inside without my noticing, and I had enough sense not to ask. I nodded to them briefly, careful not to appear in any way impressed, because I knew Johnny was only waiting for a chance to be insufferably proud of himself. I looked at Annie, and she sighed and threw herself on the sword.

'I didn't see either of you arrive.'

'No one ever does!' Johnny said smugly. 'Unless I want them to. I walk unseen in the world and tap-dance between the raindrops, just because I can. And because I have to do something to take my mind off things.'

'What things?' I said before I could stop myself.

'Don't ask,' said Johnny.

'You're starting to sound like Lex,' I said. 'He's always been a great one for the gnomic utterance.'

Johnny beamed at the Damned, who was sitting stiffly on the seat beside him. 'It turns out we have a lot in common. Both of us academics, who would have been perfectly happy to stay in our ivory towers . . . but we were seduced out into the real world and punished by what we found waiting for us there. We've spent the day visiting low dives, getting in and out of trouble, and talking about life and death and similar things.'

'It's been a long time since I had someone I could talk to,' said Lex. 'At least, someone who didn't want something from me. Or ended up running away screaming.'

Johnny patted him encouragingly on the shoulder. 'Stick with me, kid; I'll make you a star.'

'Can we please get a move on?' said Annie. 'It's a cold evening to be standing around in an iconic white dress.'

'We can't go anywhere without the Ghost,' I said.

'I'm right here,' he said.

I looked up to where the Ghost was sitting cross-legged on the roof of my car. He was wearing the memories of old motorcycle leathers, complete with racing goggles perched on his forehead. I had to fight down an urge to sigh deeply.

'What are you doing up there?'

'It's too crowded in the back seat,' said the Ghost. 'I'd end up overlapping Lex and Johnny, and I hate it when that happens. It makes me feel less real. I'm fine up here. You can drive as fast as you like and it won't bother me.'

Lex and Johnny stuck their heads out of the car's side windows, so they could check out who I was talking to. The Ghost waved at them cheerfully. Johnny and Lex pulled their heads back in and looked at each other.

'I didn't see him get up there,' said Lex. 'Did you see him get up there, Johnny?'

'No,' said the Wild Card. 'Which is actually kind of spooky.'

'The man who can be anywhere,' said Lex. 'Just what we need on a mission like this.'

'Is he, strictly speaking, still a man?' said Johnny.

'I heard that!' the Ghost said loudly. 'Don't make me come down there and haunt you.'

'He does that spooky voice very well, doesn't he?' said Johnny.

'I've got chills,' said Lex.

I got into the car and revved the engine loudly. Because I just knew that if I let them, they'd keep up this nonsense for hours. Annie dropped into the passenger seat and arranged herself decorously beside me. I put the car in gear, and we set off at speed for the bright lights of London.

A car full of weird, with a ghost on top.

It was ten o'clock in the evening, and the gaudy neon was working overtime when we finally arrived at Oxford Street. People swarmed up and down the pavements, alert for anything that might turn out to be a good time, while the traffic did its usual spiteful best to obstruct and delay us. But we still got there in plenty of time, because every single traffic light turned green the moment we approached – just to please Annie. She slumped down in her seat and pretended she hadn't noticed. Lex and Johnny found it endlessly amusing, so I had to act as if I didn't. The Ghost slammed his fists on the roof of the car every time we slowed down, and demanded to know what was happening. I ignored him.

I finally reduced our speed to a crawl, so I could check out the shops we were passing. While studiously ignoring the increasingly loud complaints from the traffic piling up behind us.

'You have been to this pizza place before, haven't you?' said Annie after a while.

'Just the once,' I said. 'I took a quick look from a distance and then moved on before anyone had a chance to notice I was interested. When you're messing with Hammer's business, you never know who might be watching. I'm sure it was along here somewhere . . . Ah! Yes! Here we are!'

I slammed on the brakes and brought the car to a halt right outside the Perfect Pizza Palace. I got out and went round to open the door for Annie, ignoring the symphony of aggrieved car horns from all sides, and any number of angry comments from passing taxi drivers. Annie emerged from the car like a starlet on opening night and fussily smoothed down her dress with both hands. An awful lot of people stopped to watch her, and Annie smiled at me triumphantly. I nodded, acknowledging the point.

Lex and Johnny erupted from the car like clowns in a circus act, doing an extended *No, after you, I insist* routine until I felt like throwing things at them. They only broke off when the Ghost sank magisterially down through the roof of the car, without changing his position, and finally walked casually through the side of the car to join us.

'Now that's just showing off,' said Johnny.

'You should know,' said the Ghost.

'You are aware you've parked on a double yellow line, Gideon?' said Annie. 'Right in the middle of one of the busiest streets in London?'

I just shrugged and smiled. 'If the car is still here when we get back, fine. If it's gone, or clamped, then to hell with it. We'll just hail a taxi, because when we get back, we'll be able to afford one.'

'And while taxi drivers might not stop for someone who looks like the Damned, they'll definitely stop for Marilyn,' said Annie.

I let her have that one and took a moment to check I had all my special gadgets tucked safely away about my person. The pen that could put Time on pause, the skeleton key that could unlock anything, and the compass that would always point to what I needed.

'You do have very nice toys, Gideon,' said Lex. 'However, Johnny and I have been wondering . . . We all bring our own special gifts to this crew, but what gift do you bring?'

'The gift of putting together a really good crew,' I said. I looked at the Damned and the Wild Card, the Ghost and Annie Anybody, and couldn't keep from grinning. 'It's us against the world. And the world had better watch out.'

I led the way into the Perfect Pizza Palace, which wasn't nearly as palatial as its name suggested. In fact, it would have needed a major upgrade to qualify as a dump. A hygiene inspector would have condemned the place on sight, and judging by the decor, the taste police had never been allowed in. There were a few customers, sitting glumly at their tables, but none of them paid us any attention.

'What a dump,' said Lex.

'I thought that,' I said.

'Maybe the setting makes the food taste better by comparison,' said Johnny.

'No food could taste that good,' said Lex.

'I'm surprised it's still open, this late in the evening,' said Annie.

'Hammer owns the place,' I said. 'He makes sure it stays open all hours, so his people will always have access to the dimensional door.'

'I'm not seeing any guards,' said Lex. 'I was sure there'd be guards.'

'Who do you think those are, pretending to be customers?' I said.

'I used to be very fond of pizza,' said the Ghost. 'At least, I think I did. Pizza is the flat one, right?'

Johnny patted the Ghost comfortingly on his shoulder, and I was a little surprised to notice his hand didn't sink even a little way into the Ghost's immaterial form. Suggesting that at least one of them was more real than he cared to admit.

The staff were all lounging together by the kitchen door, so bored they couldn't even be bothered to chat, and none of them so much as glanced in our direction, let alone bustled over to threaten us with a menu. I gestured for the crew to make sure they stuck close to Johnny, as I led the way to the back of the room, trusting the Wild Card's uncertain nature to keep us hidden.

'There are hidden security cameras all over the place,' Annie said quietly. 'Along with motion trackers and infra-red scanners. I've charmed them all into editing our images out of their reports.' She smiled briefly. 'All the cameras say I look very nice as Marilyn.'

'It would seem your gift is working well,' I said diplomatically.

We finally reached the toilets at the back of the room, and I reached out to open the men's door, only to pause when I realized Annie had stopped dead in her tracks and was scowling fiercely.

'What?' I said politely.

'Are you kidding me?' she said harshly. 'I thought I'd reached the bottom of my career, but this is a new low. Sneaking into a men's toilet . . . I'm going to get my shoes wet, aren't I? Oh, God, I can smell the state of the place even through the closed door.'

'No, you can't,' I said. 'Get in there.'

I opened the door and pushed Annie through, and the rest of us crowded in after her before she could get out again. The toilet was empty, and, if anything, looked cleaner than the dining area. The air smelled strongly of something like pine. I looked around for the dimensional door, but the only actual door was the one we'd just come through. Lex moved quickly down the row of cubicles, slamming their doors open one after the other to make sure they were empty, until he got to the last one and found a door that wouldn't budge.

'Don't worry; it's empty,' said Johnny.

'Don't ask him how he knows that,' said Lex.

'I am wise and wonderful and know many things,' Johnny said happily.

'And you can see round corners,' the Ghost said crushingly.

I got out my compass and the needle pointed unerringly at the closed cubicle door. We all moved over to stand before it and consider the door carefully.

'What do you want to bet that the only way to work the dimensional door is by sitting on the toilet and pulling the chain?' said Annie.

'Why do you always have to go straight to the worst-case scenario?' I said.

'Years of experience,' said Annie. 'A lot of them working with you.'

'Do you want me to break the door in?' said Lex.

'Better not,' I said. 'We don't want to risk damaging anything.'

I put my compass away, took out my skeleton key and pointed it at the cubicle door. I turned the key carefully in mid-air and the cubicle door unlocked itself. I gave it a gentle push and the door fell back slowly, revealing nothing but an impenetrable darkness, as though the cubicle was full of night. I remembered a similar darkness inside the Box of Beyond and repressed a shudder. Annie squeezed in beside me and sniffed loudly, to show just how unimpressed she was.

'So . . . do we think this is a good or a bad thing?'

'It's just a simple camouflage spell,' said Johnny. 'Like graffiti scrawled over reality. We won't be able to see what's really in there until we go through.'

'Are we actually going to trust the crazy guy on this?' said Annie.

Johnny looked around the toilet. 'What crazy guy?'

'Is everybody ready?' I said.

None of them said anything. They all stood shoulder to shoulder, crowded together, staring silently into the dark, caught up in the enormity of what we were about to do. Fortunately, I had something with me I'd prepared earlier, just in case I needed to lighten the mood. I took out my black domino burglar's mask, put it on and struck a dramatic pose.

'How do I look?'

'Like someone way out of their depth, in a mask,' said the Ghost.

Everyone had some kind of smile on their face, so I seized the moment and marched straight into the dark of the cubicle, and the others followed me in.

There was barely a moment's transition before bright light filled my eyes, and we were all suddenly standing in a cavern the size of several football stadiums. The scale was staggering, as though we'd left the world we knew for something bigger. It was a moment before I could tear my gaze away and glance behind me, and my heart lurched suddenly as it missed a beat. The dimensional door had disappeared. There was nothing behind us but a whole lot of empty space. I must have made some kind of noise, because everyone else turned to look at what I wasn't seeing. I felt a little reassured when they all made their own noises. Apart from the Wild Card, of course.

'Will you please stop panicking?' said Johnny. 'It's far too early for that. This is all perfectly normal. Most dimensional doors have only got one side; that's how they work.'

I reached out a hand and was quietly very relieved when my fingertips stubbed up against the unseen door. I looked down and saw that someone had carved a cross deep into the stone of the cavern floor, to mark the dimensional door's position. Presumably, so that Hammer's people could always be sure of finding it when they needed to leave. I drew everyone's attention to the cross on the ground.

'Look around, people, and find some landmark you'll remember. Just in case you need to find this spot again in a hurry. If anything should go wrong, and we get separated, this is the way out.'

'How can anything possibly go wrong?' said Annie. 'You're wearing an official burglar's mask.'

'It's nice that you still have so much confidence in me,' I said.

'I can see the door!' Johnny said brightly.

'Of course you can,' said Annie.

'Sorry,' Johnny said meanly, 'who are you supposed to be, again?'

'Let's get moving,' I said quickly.

We started off across the great open floor. I was still amazed and awed by the sheer size of the cavern. Back in the morning of the world, some geological event must have blown a really big bubble in the earth. The roof was so far above us that I was surprised there weren't clouds floating about, and the walls were sparkling with mineral seams and strange crystal growths. I could see all of this perfectly clearly because of the fierce electrical lights hanging off huge steel pylons set up all over the cavern, illuminating the whole area as bright as day.

Gnarled stalactites hung down from the ceiling, like sleeping gargoyles. Equally misshapen stalagmites thrust up from the cavern floor, along with dozens of huge standing stones, like the monoliths of Stonehenge. Except no one had bothered to arrange these stones in pleasing patterns. Even so, they had to have been placed there deliberately, for reasons or rituals beyond our modern understanding. The monoliths themselves were just rough stone, shaped rather than carved, each of them twice the size of a man. I didn't know why I thought that; there was nothing human about them.

There was a definite presence to the place, as though we were walking through an ancient underground cathedral.

'Well,' I said, thinking I should say something, 'if nothing else, it would appear there are things we can use for cover if we have to.'

'You had to look on the bright side, didn't you?' said Lex.

'He just can't help himself,' said Annie. 'You have no idea how much that will come to grate on your nerves.'

'Confidence can be very irritating,' said Johnny. 'To those of us cursed to see things as they really are.'

'Johnny, we talked about this,' Lex said quietly. 'Outside voice, inside voice – remember?'

Annie shot me a thoughtful look. 'Why didn't they put the dimensional door closer to the museum?'

'I don't know,' I said. 'Probably so the surveillance systems could get a good look at everyone who approaches.'

'And why didn't Sable's book mention all these standing stones?' said Annie. 'I mean, how could he have missed them?'

'The book doesn't mention everything,' I said patiently. 'Just what's necessary to run the heist.'

'I'm getting a bad feeling about this place,' said the Ghost.

'Of course you are,' said Lex. 'Hammer lives here.'

'No . . . that's not it,' said the Ghost.

'There!' I said, pointing ahead. 'Hammer's idea of Heaven on earth.'

The museum was a grim, forbidding structure with no style or aesthetic to it at all. Just a great concrete bunker, with no breaks in the walls and only the one door, which looked as if it had been fashioned from solid steel. A wild variety of electronic equipment crawled over the exterior like technological ivy, and there were so many weapon emplacements on the flat roof they almost crowded each other off the edges. The long barrels moved through slow tracking routines as they covered every possible approach to the museum.

Actually, everything about the building felt like staring down the barrel of a gun.

'I don't know much about guns,' the Ghost said diffidently. 'What kind are those?'

'The kind that can not only kill you but also make a real mess of your surroundings,' I said. 'So let's not do anything to attract their attention.'

'Relax,' said Annie. 'I've already charmed their computer targeting systems into not seeing us or announcing our arrival. And I've done the same thing with the museum's security systems, so no one has any idea that we're here.'

'I knew you'd come in handy,' I said.

'I'm amazed you can function at all without me,' said Annie.

'We still have to cross a lot of open ground, people,' said Lex.

'Just as well the museum doesn't have any windows, then,' I said.

'Major design flaw,' said the Ghost. 'What were they thinking?'

'I'm not seeing any of the defences the book described,' said Lex. 'And I'm starting to think that might not be a good thing.'

'We're definitely not alone here,' said the Ghost.

We all looked at him, but he had nothing more to say.

I turned to the Wild Card. 'OK, Johnny, do your thing.'

'How do you mean?' he said.

I stopped dead in my tracks to look at him, and everyone else stopped with me.

'Use your uncertain nature to hide us, so we can start the plan,' I said carefully.

'How am I supposed to do that?' said Johnny. 'My unique nature only works on people, not things. The effect I have on the world is a consequence of what I am, not what I can do.'

'Oh . . . shit,' I said.

'That's it?' said Lex. 'Your great plan has gone wrong already?'

He glared about him, his hands clenched into fists, ready to take on anything that moved.

'Easy, big boy,' I said. 'We're not in any danger just yet. See how still and quiet everything is?'

'I did warn you not to depend on me,' Johnny said sadly.

'It's not your fault,' said Lex.

'That would make a nice change,' said Johnny.

'What are we going to do?' said the Ghost.

I thought hard and then turned to Annie. 'Are you sure you've charmed all of the security systems?'

'It's just one big system,' said Annie. 'And right now it loves me more than life itself.'

'Weird,' said Johnny, shaking his head. 'Really weird.'

'You'd know,' Annie said coldly.

'Exactly!' said Johnny.

'Please don't upset the only member of the crew who can hide us from the weapons of mass destruction,' I said. 'And I can't believe I actually needed to say that.'

'It's just bullets,' Johnny said sulkily.

'Inside voice . . .' said Lex.

'Right now, we're completely hidden from all forms of surveillance,' said Annie. 'They're doing everything they can to please me, which is more than anyone on this crew has ever done. So even if we do have problems with Hammer's outer defences, no one inside the museum should have any idea that anything is happening.'

'I'm not feeling any poltergeist activity,' I said slowly. 'The book said we would know if the attack dogs were anywhere near. And I don't see any golem guards.'

'I'm surprised there aren't any human guards patrolling the area,' said Annie.

'Probably too dangerous for them,' said Lex. 'And there's always the chance the book could be wrong when it comes to the demon dogs. We can't depend on getting any kind of warning.'

'It's a bit late to start disbelieving the book now!' I said.

'I never trusted it,' said Lex. 'It's just someone's word, and the only thing you can be sure of with people is that they'll always let you down.'

'If you don't believe in the book, what are you doing here?' I said.

He met my gaze squarely. 'You promised me a chance for revenge on Hammer.'

'And you'll get it,' I said. 'OK, people, let's head for the museum.'

'After you,' said Annie.

'No,' said Lex. 'I go first. I have armour.'

'Don't put it on unless you absolutely have to,' I said. 'Hammer could have special measures in place, triggered to activate the moment they detect your armour.'

'They won't stop me,' said Lex. 'Nothing will. Let's go.'

'Wait a minute,' I said.

I took out my map and unfolded it, and reminded everyone of where the curses were buried.

'Look for landmarks near the safe paths,' I said. 'And fix them in your mind.'

'Why didn't you bring the journal with you?' said Annie. 'It might have had more details.'

'I couldn't risk the book falling into Hammer's hands,' I said steadily. 'So I put it back in the original Sable's safe deposit box. For some other thief to find – and work out a better plan than ours if we don't come back.'

Annie nodded slowly. 'Because hurting Hammer is what matters.'

'Yes,' said Lex, 'it is.'

'There's a safe path right in front of us, heading straight to the museum's front door,' I said. 'Just stick together, people, and we'll be fine.'

'There you go with that optimism thing again,' said Johnny.

I nodded to Lex to lead the way, and he set off along the invisible path. We all followed after him, careful to walk only where he walked. The sound of our footsteps seemed very small in the great open space, as though we were barely there.

For a long time, nothing bad happened, and I think we were all starting to relax a little when Lex got a little too close to one of the standing stones. It suddenly began to rock back and forth on its base, as though it was about to topple over. Everyone backed away, and I had to yell at them to remember the curse mines and stay on the path. The stone of the monolith cracked and splintered, as parts of it broke away to form arms and legs and a blunt head.

'It's a golem guard!' said Lex.

'We have to do something before it wakes all the other stones up,' said Johnny.

'This must have been covered in the missing pages.' I turned to Annie. 'Can you charm it?'

'My gift only works on machines!' She looked quickly around at the dozens of other stone monoliths. 'You mean all of them could be golems?'

'Wouldn't surprise me,' said Lex. 'Probably triggered by human proximity.'

'What do we do?' said the Ghost.

'I'm all for saying nuts to this and heading back to the dimensional door,' said Johnny. 'This heist went very bad, very quickly. Can't help thinking that's an omen.'

'Stand where you are, Johnny,' said Lex. 'We can handle this. Trust me.'

'You can't see what's powering them,' said the Wild Card.

'Golems usually have activating words written on their forehead,' I said. 'Wipe off the mark and the golem will stop working.'

'This one doesn't have a mark on its forehead,' said Lex. 'And even if there was a hidden mark, I still wouldn't be able to reach that high, would I?'

The golem raised a single fist, like a massive stone maul, and its blunt face turned slowly back and forth, as though uncertain who to kill first. And then it lurched forward, its stone feet pounding heavily on the cavern floor.

'Scatter!' I said. 'Don't give it a single target.'

The sheer weight of the stone golem made it ponderously slow, giving us more than enough time to spread out and form a circle around it. The golem stopped abruptly, as though unable to choose between so many targets, and Lex used that moment to put on his armour. The halos at his wrists glowed fiercely, and then the light and the dark swept over him in a moment, sealing him off from the world and all human weakness. Just like that, there was a new presence in the cavern, something so heavy it could break the world merely by walking on it.

None of us could bear to look at the armour directly. Johnny had to close his eyes and turn his head away, because he could see what the armour really was.

The golem guard went straight for Lex, its blunt stone feet slamming down on the cavern floor. Clouds of dust flew up with every impact. The golem loomed over Lex and raised its massive stone fist. The Damned stood his ground, motionless as a statue. The fist came down like a hammer and shattered into pieces against Lex's armoured head. The golem stopped and looked at the broken stone where its hand used to be, as though this eventuality hadn't been covered in its operating instructions. Lex took a step forward, and the golem fell back a step. Lex went for it.

I couldn't see his face inside the armour, but I just knew he was smiling his terrible cold smile, relishing the chance to strike back at Hammer, even if only indirectly.

Lex punched the golem in its stone chest with incredible force, and jagged cracks radiated out from the blow, but the golem didn't break apart and it didn't fall. Instead, it grabbed Lex by the shoulder with its one remaining hand, to pull him forward into its embrace. Lex dug his armoured heels into the cavern floor, but they just left runnels in the dusty stone as he was dragged forward anyway. Lex stopped fighting the pull and moved in close with the golem, doing his best to wrestle with it. He set his armoured arms against the guard, straining furiously, but the golem's sheer inertia made it hard to move or resist.

'Lex!' I said suddenly. 'I've got an idea!'

'Better be a good one,' he said, not looking round as he fought to hold off the golem's relentless strength. 'This overactive boulder doesn't seem to have any weak spots.'

'There's a buried curse, about ten feet to your left,' I said. 'Throw the golem at it!'

Lex broke the thing's hold with an effort, grabbed the stone shape and lifted it off its feet. I pointed at the nearest buried curse, and Lex hurled the golem on to it. There was a sharp flash of light, and the golem melted down into a pool of bubbling magma. I winced away from the terrible heat coming off it, even at a distance.

Annie and the Ghost looked quickly around for more stone guards, while Johnny looked thoughtfully at what had been a golem guard. I glanced at the museum, but there was nothing to indicate they'd heard anything.

'You'd better lose the armour, Lex,' I said. 'Just in case.'

The light and the dark disappeared in a moment, and Lex reappeared. He flinched back a step, as the heat from the magma hit him.

'Hot time in the old cavern tonight,' he said solemnly.

'The whole of the cavern floor is covered with these Trojan golems,' said Annie. 'The sneaky bastards.'

'This is Fredric Hammer's domain,' said the Ghost. 'We must have been mad to think we could take him on his own territory.'

'Just because we're mad, doesn't mean we can't win,' Johnny said reasonably.

'We go on,' I said. 'Keep to the safe path and stay away from the standing stones, and we should be fine. Lex, lead the way.'

He didn't even look at me, just headed straight for the museum. And we went after him.

The cavern was almost unbearably still, as though everything was holding its breath to see what would happen next. The blind concrete walls of the museum drew steadily closer, and then Lex stopped abruptly and looked off to one side, frowning, as though struggling to make out something. We all stopped with him and looked where he was looking, but there was nothing there.

I moved in beside him. 'What is it, Lex?'

'There's something up ahead, to one side,' he said quietly. 'It feels like the tension you get on the air just before a storm breaks.'

'It's the poltergeist attack dogs,' said Johnny.

We all looked at him.

'How can you be sure?' said Annie.

'Because I can see them,' said Johnny.

I strained my eyes but still couldn't see or feel anything. The Ghost looked uneasy, and Annie was trying to look in every direction at once. I turned back to Lex.

'What are you seeing, exactly?'

'It's like a mirage on the air, only without the mirage,' he said slowly. 'A disturbance in the way things should be. Whatever it is, it's getting closer. I think it knows we know it's there. How am I supposed to fight something I can't even see?'

'Allow me,' said Johnny.

He snapped his fingers at the way ahead of us, and three poltergeist attack dogs appeared out of nowhere. Dark swirling clouds of elemental energies, shot through with flashes of lightning, radiating hostility. All three of them bumped along the cavern floor, heading straight for us.

'Now you're seeing the world the way I do,' said the Wild Card. 'Can you honestly say you're any happier for it?'

The attack dogs surged forward, as though they'd picked up our scent. I could feel their presence now, like fingernails scraping down the blackboard of my soul.

Annie stepped behind me and peered over my shoulder. 'How dangerous are those things?'

'According to Sable's journal, very,' I said steadily. 'The forces they control could tear us apart in a moment.'

'Wasn't there anything in the book about how to deal with these things?'

'Yes,' I said. 'Set the Ghost on them.'

'Right,' the Ghost said happily. 'Not a problem.'

He strode forward to confront the approaching entities, and we all stayed exactly where we were and let him do it.

'I've seen things like this before,' the Ghost said over his shoulder. 'When the book called them poltergeist attack dogs, I was expecting some kind of demon . . . But this is just spiritual bad weather, given shape and a purpose. Nothing at all to worry about.'

He walked right up to the spitting, crackling energy things, and all three of them slammed to a halt. The Ghost glared at them, and his presence suddenly became unbearable. Death was with us, blunt and uncompromising. The end of all things in a human shape.

Lex's halos sparked and sputtered at his wrists, uncertain whether to manifest his armour. Johnny was frowning, as though seeing something unexpected for the first time in ages and not liking it. Annie grabbed hold of my arm with both hands. I put a hand on top of hers and hoped I'd been right about the Ghost.

The poltergeist attack dogs retreated quickly in the face of something they couldn't bear, disappearing as they went. Because they couldn't stand to exist after what they'd been shown. Once they were gone, the Ghost turned back to face us, and once again he was just the friendly figure we'd thought we knew. It was easy to forget, sometimes, that he really was dead and all that such a thing entailed.

'They were only guard dogs,' he said mildly. 'And dogs have always been frightened of me. I don't know why.'

I just nodded. I wasn't going to be the one to tell him. I turned to Lex.

'The longer we spend out here, the more chance we'll run into something we can't handle. You'd better run interference and get us to the museum as quickly as possible.'

'No,' the Ghost said sharply. 'I should go first, because I can see where the curses are buried. I can see other things, too. So much is becoming clearer to me now . . . as though I've been asleep and dreaming.'

'All right,' I said. 'You're on. Everyone else, stay close. Annie, you can let go of my arm now.'

She quickly took her hands away, not looking at me. The Ghost set off towards the museum, and we all followed him. And that was when every single stone monolith suddenly woke up. Jagged cracks split and splintered the solid stone as they took on their human shapes, and then they all came lurching forward from every direction at once to block our way and surround us. The Ghost stopped, and we all stopped with him.

'Did I do that?' he said. 'I didn't mean to do that.'

'They must have been triggered when we got too close to the museum,' I said. 'An army of unbeatable, undying guards . . .'

'You must have a plan!' said Annie. 'You always have a plan!'

'Just the one,' I said. I took out my ballpoint pen. 'Grab hold of my arm again, Annie, and hold your breath.'

We both took a deep breath, and I hit the button on the pen. Time crashed to a halt, just for the two of us. The world took on a deep reddish tinge, as though the pen had slowed down light itself, and all sound stopped. In the eerie silence of the unmoving world, a glance at the map showed that all of the golem guards had frozen in place. I indicated to Annie the guns on top of the museum, and she nodded quickly but gestured back at me that we'd have to get a lot closer before she could take control of their computer targeting systems. It was good to know the old mind-reading connection was still there. We pressed forward together, forcing our way through a world that resisted our every movement, both of us already desperate for air that wasn't there.

The museum seemed impossibly far away. Every step was an effort, every foot gained a struggle. The world did everything it could to hold us back, but we wouldn't be stopped. Annie stuck close beside me, matching me step for step, and her strength gave me strength. We had to get all the way to the front door before Annie indicated we were close enough and I could hit the button again. We crashed back into Time, gasping for breath and leaning on each other for support. I gestured urgently at the roof, and Annie seized control of the guns. The long barrels whined loudly as they changed position, locking on to new targets. And then they all fired at once, and every single golem guard was blown into a hundred pieces.

The rest of the crew all but jumped out of their skins, as the rain of pebbles fell to the cavern floor. And then they almost did it again when they realized Annie and I weren't where we had been just a moment before. I motioned for them to come and join us, and they hurried forward.

'You used the pen, didn't you?' said Johnny. 'You must let me try that some time.'

'You're dangerous enough as it is,' I said.

Johnny beamed at me. 'Why, thank you, Gideon. That's the nicest thing you've ever said about me.'

I couldn't believe no one inside the museum had heard all the guns firing at once. The concrete walls must be really thick. I looked back across the cavern, at all the ground we'd covered and the threats we'd faced, and grinned suddenly.

'What?' said Lex.

'This was supposed to be the easy part . . .' I said.

'What do we do now?' said Johnny, looking interestedly at the solid steel front door. 'Knock loudly and tell them we're carol singers?'

'Hush,' I said. 'I'm thinking.'

'Can't you open it with your skeleton key?' said Annie.

'First things first,' I said. 'Ghost, I need you to stick your head through that door and tell us what's on the other side.'

The Ghost looked at me and then at the door. 'I don't like to. What if there's something nasty waiting? What if it grabs hold of my head and rips it off?'

I looked at him. 'How likely is that?'

'There might be,' said the Ghost. 'You don't know. I have to think about things like this, because no one else will.'

'Ghost,' I said, with great patience, 'there is no one waiting on the other side of this door. The book says so.'

'Then why do you need me to take a look?' the Ghost said craftily.

'Because I need to be sure!'

The Ghost sighed loudly, which was just a bit disconcerting, coming from someone who didn't need to breathe.

'All right, I'll walk through the door and take a quick look.' He started forward and then stopped again, looking closely at the door. 'Unless this has been specially booby-trapped to do nasty things to ghosts when they try to get in. That's what I'd do if I were Hammer.'

'You weren't bothered by the poltergeist attack dogs, but you're worried about a door?' said Annie.

'Welcome to my world,' said the Ghost.

'Get in there,' I said. 'Or I'll reverse the polarity of your ectoplasm.'

'Bully.'

He walked through the steel door and disappeared. There was a pause and then he stuck his head back out, like an unpleasant hunting trophy.

'The coast is clear. Come on in.'

He pulled his head back. I opened the door with my skeleton key, and – just like that – we were all safely inside the fortress of the most dangerous man in the world.

TWELVE

In the Lair of the Beast
Expect the Unexpected

The hallway was completely empty, just as it was supposed to be. It was all bare walls and stark fluorescent lighting, with no fittings or furnishings, or even a hint of comfort. More like the entrance to a barracks than a museum. Lex started to say something, and I got right in his face to hush him.

'Now we're inside, we can be heard,' I said quietly but firmly. 'So keep your voice down.'

Lex looked as if he was going to say something anyway, but Annie beat him to it.

'How can Hammer bear to live in a place like this? I was expecting something more . . . luxurious.'

'He lives here because this is where his collection is,' I said. 'I don't think he cares about anything else.'

'Oh, that's sad,' said the Ghost, just a bit unexpectedly. 'What good does it do to own the whole world if you've lost your appreciation for it?'

'Was that a quote?' said Lex.

'Very nearly,' said Johnny.

'Can't we all just agree the man is a monster and move on?' said Annie. 'I really don't like standing around here.'

'Is your gift still working?' I said. 'Are the interior security systems thoroughly charmed?'

'Of course,' said Annie. 'Otherwise, it would be all bells and sirens and flashing lights, and men with big guns come to say hello.' She paused, her head cocked slightly to one side. 'I can hear some of the systems chattering away in the background. They keep asking if there's anything more they can do for me. There's a reason I like machines more than people.'

'Weird,' said Johnny, shaking his head sadly.

Annie glared at him coldly. 'You really are pushing it.'

He beamed at her. 'I am, aren't I?'

'This is where I say goodbye,' Lex said abruptly.

We all turned to look at him. He was staring off down the empty hallway, and more than ever his face looked as though it had been carved out of stone, harsh and uncompromising.

'You can't just go rushing off,' I said. 'We have to follow the plan as it's laid down in the book if we're to avoid being noticed.'

'I don't care about the heist,' said Lex. 'I never did. I'm going to find Fredric Hammer and kill him.'

'You can't,' I said bluntly. 'The moment anyone sees you, we're all in danger. And anyway, what makes you think you could get to Hammer, past all the guards he has here?'

Lex smiled slowly, and it was a cold bitter thing. 'When I'm in my armour, it will take more than men with guns to stop me.'

'Depends on the kind of ammunition they're using,' I said. 'You of all people should know there's a bullet for everything. But it's far more likely that they'd just throw people at you, to slow you down, while Hammer made his escape. Doesn't that sound like something he'd do?'

'And besides,' said Johnny, 'you wouldn't just go off and abandon me, Lex, would you?'

Lex sighed slowly. 'You don't care about anything but the heist,' he said, not looking at anyone in particular.

'I told you at the start,' I said. 'Our only real chance for revenge on Hammer is to hurt him, not kill him.'

Lex nodded, reluctantly. 'You ask me to do the hardest things . . .'

'Only because I know you can deliver,' I said. 'And don't forget the Santa Clara Formulation, down in Hammer's vault. An immortality drug is the one thing that might free you from Hell's grasp.'

Lex almost smiled a real smile. 'Get thee behind me, Gideon.'

'Nice to see that sanity and common sense are back in the saddle,' said Annie. 'The heist is back on! How do we do this, Gideon?'

I took out a list I'd made, carefully copied from the original Sable's book. All the surreptitious moves that would hide us from everyone as we passed through the museum. While I refreshed my memory, Annie moved in close and murmured in my ear.

'Judi Rifkin seemed very sure there isn't any of the immortality drug left. What are you going to do when Lex finds out you've conned him?'

'I have decided not to think about that for the moment,' I said, just as quietly. 'Not when I have so many other worrying things to obsess over.'

'I don't like this place,' said the Ghost.

'Of course you don't,' said Lex. 'Hammer lives here.'

'No,' said the Ghost. 'That's not it. It feels like there's something strange, lurking in the background . . . Not dead and not alive, but it knows we're here.'

We all looked at him, and then the rest of the crew looked at me.

'There isn't anything like that mentioned in the book,' I said carefully. 'What do you think it might be, Ghost?'

'I have no idea.' The Ghost sounded as though that worried him. 'I've never felt anything like it before. And I've been around.'

'Well, whatever it is, it'll just have to wait,' I said. 'We've used up all the time the book allowed for us to be here. We have to get moving.'

'We were allowed time here?' said Annie.

'Why else do you think I let you stand around talking?' I said. 'Sable saw us here, on the television screen. But he also saw a guard heading this way, so we have to go and be somewhere else. Right now.'

'He knew we'd be carrying out this heist, and not him?' said Lex.

'Try not to think about it too much,' I said. 'It'll only make your head hurt.'

'What did Sable say happens after we get into the vault?' said Annie.

'If he knew, he didn't write it down. Now let's go find the vault before Hammer decides to have a garage sale just to spite us.'

I led my crew through the museum as quickly as I could, slipping quietly from one empty corridor to another, popping in and out of empty rooms and lurking behind closed doors as guards passed by. At least, I heard their voices and their footsteps; I never saw any of them because I always timed it just right. Even so, there were occasions when we only made it to a safe haven by the skin of our teeth. At one point, we all ended up crammed together in a pokey little office, as two guards held a bored conversation on the other side of the door. They finally moved on, but I made the crew wait until I'd heard their footsteps disappear into the distance.

'This is really undignified,' said Lex to the back of my neck.

'Do you want dignity or revenge?' I said. Not looking back at him, because there wasn't enough room to turn round.

'Both,' said Lex in his coldest voice.

'Well, that's just greedy,' said the Ghost.

He was hovering right in the middle of us, overlapped by everyone but trying hard to be a good sport about it.

'This is all such fun!' said Johnny. 'It's been ages since I played Sardines. Of course, back then the other side didn't get to kill you if they found you. Mostly.'

I let them out of the room and got them moving again. Several corridors later, we ended up in a room full of art. I checked my watch and told the crew they had time for a little look round, while we waited for the way ahead to clear. All four walls were covered in paintings, everything from oversized portraits to delicate miniatures. Annie moved quickly from one piece to the next, full of enthusiasm and even a little awe.

'This is one hell of a collection!' she said breathlessly. 'I mean, it's all important work, by famous names, but nothing here has ever appeared in an official catalogue, never mind a proper museum. Hammer has been hoarding masterpieces in private, just so he could gloat over them, all by himself.'

'Of course he has,' I said. 'That's what he does.'

'Take a look at this,' said Johnny. 'The Mona Lisa – naked.'

So, of course, we all had to go and take a look. Annie sniffed loudly, in a *Men!* kind of way, but she couldn't stay away either. It really was the Mona Lisa, just as we knew her – same pose, same enigmatic smile, but not a stitch of clothing to be seen anywhere.

'Must have been a private commission,' said Lex.

'This can't be a real da Vinci!' said Annie.

'Oh, yes, it is,' said the Ghost. 'I know his style, right down to the brushstrokes. I should do; I've copied it often enough.'

'He wouldn't have lowered himself,' said Annie.

'He would, for the right price,' said the Ghost. 'They all had to please their patrons first, in those days, and the real money has always been in the dodgy stuff.'

'Men!' said Annie. 'And I use the term loosely.'

She turned her back on the nude and moved away to take a close look at the miniatures. I went quickly after her.

'You keep your hands to yourself,' I said sternly. 'All it would take is for someone to come in here after we're gone and notice something is missing, and they'd raise the alarm. If you want to pick up a few souvenirs of your time here, wait till we hit the vault. Where there's bound to be a much better selection.'

'You're always so practical, Gideon,' said Annie.

'One of us has to be.'

'How much longer do we have to wait in here?' growled Lex.

I checked my watch. 'Time's almost up. All we have to do now is nip down the corridor to the room at the end and then look for a hidden door, with steps leading down to the vault.'

'Where do we look for this door?' said Lex.

'I don't know,' I said. 'I told you: it's hidden. But Sable says it's there, so it must be.'

Annie frowned. 'Why couldn't he see it on the television?'

'It must be very well hidden,' I said.

Johnny smiled mischievously at the Ghost. 'Why don't you just float down through the building and find it for us?'

'Not a good idea,' I said quickly. 'Who knows what kind of specialized sensors Hammer will have put in place, the closer we get to the vault. We do this by the book.'

'Boring,' said Johnny.

'Practical,' said Lex.

'Same thing,' said Johnny.

I eased the door open, checked the coast was clear and rushed everyone down the next corridor and into the end room. Which turned out to be full of antique clocks and precious timepieces. It seemed Hammer had a fondness for themed rooms. Unfortunately, the hidden door remained stubbornly elusive. After we'd all spent some time searching for it, and got nowhere,

I took my list out and checked it again, just in case I'd missed something.

Johnny went into ecstatics over a candle with the hours marked on it, which had once belonged to the Venerable Bede.

'This is history!' he said happily.

'What about this?' said Lex. 'A gold pocket watch that belonged to Jack the Ripper.'

We all stopped what we were doing and went to take a look. The watch had been neatly laid out on a black velvet cushion. It looked perfectly ordinary.

'The Ripper?' I said. 'Really?'

'That's what it says on the card,' said Lex.

'I suppose even infamous serial killers feel the need to be on time,' said Johnny.

'Does the card say who he was?' said Annie.

'No,' said Lex.

'Is that a spot of dried blood on the chain?' said the Ghost.

Johnny's attention had already been distracted by a nearby Rolex with strange markings on its face.

'I've seen one of these before!' he said excitedly. 'This is what Time Agents use when they travel back and forth through history.'

'You have got to be kidding,' said Annie, moving quickly over to stare at it.

'I've seen things you wouldn't believe,' Johnny said loftily. 'Some of them I don't even believe myself and I was there when they happened. Or at least I might have been – it's so hard to be sure.'

Before I could stop her, Annie picked up the Rolex and had its back off. The watch was empty.

'Just as well,' Johnny said wisely. 'Can you imagine how dangerous Hammer would be if he had control over Time?'

'Who are these Time Agents?' said Annie, putting the Rolex back where she'd found it.

'No one knows,' said Johnny. 'No one has ever survived meeting them.'

'Then how does anyone know they exist?' I said reasonably.

Johnny scowled at me. 'Don't you have a hidden door to look for?'

We searched the room again, very thoroughly, even tapping the walls and checking the floor for a trapdoor.

'Hey!' Annie said suddenly. 'Why don't you use your compass, Gideon?'

'Ah . . .' I said.

'You'd forgotten all about it, hadn't you?' said Annie.

'I've had a lot on my mind,' I said, with as much dignity as I could muster.

'Give me strength . . .' Lex muttered. Johnny laughed at me soundlessly, and the Ghost kindly pretended to be interested in something else.

The compass needle pointed unerringly at an oversized Grandfather clock. It had been built to look like a coffin, with a gap in the lid to show the clock face. I pulled back the lid, and there was the hidden door. I opened it with my skeleton key and surprised a security guard having a crafty cigarette break. He was already going for the gun at his side when Annie pushed past me and struck her best Marilyn pose. She smiled sweetly at the guard, and he just stood there and stared at her. While he was busy doing that, Lex snatched up a steel-bound alarm clock and threw it at him. The heavy object bounced off the guard's forehead and he took no further interest in the proceedings.

Lex helped me drag the guard into a corner, out of the way. By the time he woke up, we would be long gone. And the only one of us he'd be able to describe would be Marilyn Monroe. I smiled at Annie.

'All right, I was wrong.'

She smiled back at me. 'This whole journey was worth it, just to hear you say that.'

The door in the clock gave access to a set of bare stone steps, heading down into darkness, with not even a hint of light at the bottom.

'This is it, people,' I said. 'Next stop: Hammer's treasure vault.'

'It's about time,' said Johnny.

The steps dropped away into darkness for ages, but automatic lights constantly turned themselves on and off, so that we were always moving in a pool of light. The steps finally ended before a massive steel slab, with no obvious lock or handle.

'We're here,' I said. 'Everything we ever dreamed of stealing is on the other side of this door.'

'Looks very solid, doesn't it?' said Johnny.

I nodded to the Ghost. 'Do your party trick again. Walk through that door and make sure the time television is still there.'

The Ghost looked suspiciously at the door. 'I've got that bad feeling again – only worse. The not-dead-and-not-alive thing is waiting for us, inside the vault.'

'If that's the strangest thing Hammer has in his collection, I'll be surprised,' I said. 'Come on, Ghost; we have to get in there.'

'Yes, we do,' the Ghost said unhappily. 'We need to know what this thing is.'

He strode through the steel door and disappeared.

'I didn't think he'd agree that easily,' I said. 'I had a whole bunch of good arguments lined up to convince him, and he never gave me a chance to use any of them.'

'He's selfish like that,' said Johnny.

There was a worryingly long pause, and then the Ghost walked back through the steel door, shaking his head.

'You are not going to believe what Hammer's got in there . . .'

'Is it a treasure house?' said Annie.

'All of that and more,' said the Ghost.

'Did you see the television?' I said.

'I couldn't see it anywhere,' said the Ghost. 'The vault is packed with amazing things, but none of them have been properly set out or displayed. They've just been . . . dumped in piles, or left to fend for themselves. There are only a few passageways left open for us to walk through.'

'That's all we'll need,' I said.

I got out my skeleton key, pointed it at the steel door and turned it slowly, and the massive steel door made loud clunking noises as heavy interior bolts drew back. The door swung smoothly open before us, and I led the way in, with the others crowding my heels.

The Ghost was right. Treasures and wonders beyond counting had been stacked high in tottering piles, or left to stand alone if they were too big, all under a harsh unflattering light that seemed to come from everywhere at once. I got my compass out again and followed its pointing needle into a narrow passageway.

'Does anyone else think we should be leaving a thread behind us?' said Annie.

'Maybe he's got a minotaur in here,' said the Ghost.

'That's just bullshit,' said Lex.

'Where?' said Johnny.

Tottering piles loomed over us as we made our way deeper into the labyrinth. Expensive and intriguing items had been packed tightly together to make the walls of the maze we walked through – unprotected and uncared for, like a cupboard full of junk you can't quite bring yourself to throw away. Sometimes the passageway became so narrow we had to turn sideways to keep going.

'Reminds me of a documentary I saw about hoarders,' said Annie.

I nodded slowly. 'It's as though Hammer doesn't care about anything once he's acquired it.'

'That's collectors for you,' said Johnny. 'For a lot of them, it's all about the thrill of the chase. And owning things to make sure your rivals can't have them.'

I held the compass out before me, following the pointing needle, and the crew stuck close behind me.

'We're going to have to search through a hell of a lot of stuff to find the television,' said Annie. 'How much time do we have, Gideon?'

'No one knows we're down here,' I said. 'So we don't have to worry about security. But the route back out, as described in the book, is only good for a certain period.'

'Maybe we should walk faster,' said Annie.

'Didn't the book say where to look for the television?' said Lex, scowling darkly about him.

'No,' I said. 'It must have been on one of the missing pages.'

'The ones that were deliberately torn out?' said Annie.

'Yes,' I said. 'I'm starting to think there are things about this heist that the original Sable didn't want us to know. Because if we did, we wouldn't dare try.'

Hammer's treasure vault turned out to be even bigger than the museum above it and packed with a lifetime's acquisition of everything strange under the sun and the moon. The crew kept wanting to pause and examine things, but I kept them moving, until Johnny stopped suddenly and refused to be moved.

'What is it?' said Lex.

'It's this place!' said Johnny, clapping his hands over his ears. 'It's full of voices, all of them shouting at once!'

'I don't hear anything,' Lex said carefully. 'There's no one here but us, Johnny.'

'It's the collection!' said Johnny. 'I can't hear myself think for all the noise they're making.'

'Concentrate,' said Lex. 'Remember, you don't have to let anything inside your head that you don't want there.'

Johnny nodded, breathing hard, and after a moment he lowered his hands and we moved on. But there were always some things we just had to stop and look at.

A window hovered in mid-air, showing a Venusian landscape in what looked like real time. The sky was yellow and the mountains were purple, and all the proportions and angles were subtly and horribly wrong. Something made out of thorns scuttled across a bare plain in search of shelter.

A little further on, we came to an old-fashioned electric chair. Its dangling leather restraints were frayed and worn, and there were burn marks everywhere. The Ghost stood before it, frowning thoughtfully.

'What's the matter?' I said, trying hard to sound patient.

'This chair is surrounded by the spirits of those who died in it,' said the Ghost. 'It seems Hammer acquired them when he collected the chair, and now he won't let them go. They're very angry about that.'

He started forward, but Johnny stopped him with a hand on his immaterial arm. The Ghost looked at him with something like shock.

'Those are really unquiet spirits,' said Johnny. 'You don't want anything to do with them.'

'I have to try to help,' said the Ghost.

'They won't thank you for it.'

'What's that got to do with anything?' said the Ghost.

He started speaking quietly to people only he could see, and we moved on and left him to it.

Johnny was the next to get distracted, by a human-sized puppet of Mr Punch tap-dancing endlessly in a corner. His carved wooden face was twisted by the usual rictus grin, and his eyes were full of all the malice in the world. Johnny nodded quickly, as though in response to something only he could hear, and went to talk to the puppet, shrugging off Lex's hand when he tried to stop him. They danced together, the Wild Card and the avatar of chaos, and what they had to say to each other was best not overheard.

Lex ended up standing before a huge old-fashioned freezer cabinet, held shut by several lengths of steel chain and some very heavy padlocks. He looked at me.

'Open them.'

'We're not going to find a television set inside a freezer,' I said.

'But we might find an immortality drug,' said Lex. 'Open it.'

I did the business with the skeleton key, and all the padlocks sprang open. Lex ripped the chains away and then hauled open the heavy door to reveal shelves packed with bottles and phials, and a number of human body parts inside carefully labelled plastic bags. The eyes of a famous painter, the hands of a legendary guitarist, and something not entirely unexpected from a very well-known male porn star.

'I suppose there are all kinds of collectibles,' I said. 'Hey, Ghost . . .'

He was already standing beside me when I turned round, looking distinctly upset.

'Those were very unpleasant spirits. There's never any call for that kind of language. What do you want, Gideon?'

'Are there are any ghosts connected to these bits and pieces?' I said. 'Anyone you could talk to?'

'There's nobody here,' said the Ghost. 'This is just what the dead left behind.'

And then he wandered off again.

'Why did you want to know that?' Annie said to me.

'If there were any spirits here,' I said, 'trapped by Hammer along with their remains, we might have been able to find a way to break them loose.'

Annie smiled. 'There's hope for you yet.'

Lex frowned at the rows and rows of bottles and potions. 'I'm not seeing the Santa Clara Formulation anywhere. Or anything that even looks like it might be an immortality drug.'

'Can we please not get distracted?' I said. 'Find the television first, fill our pockets later.'

Lex nodded reluctantly and slammed the freezer door shut. I looked over to where Johnny was holding the limp and lifeless figure of Mr Punch in his arms. The rictus in the wooden face had turned into a scream of horror. I wondered what Johnny had told him. Johnny dropped the puppet carelessly to the floor and came back to join us.

'Now, that is how you do it,' he said calmly.

On we went, pressing deeper into the labyrinth. We passed a ten-gallon bottle of tequila, where the worm was so big it filled half the bottle. It slowly turned its bulging head to watch us pass, dreaming in its alcohol sea.

'I wonder what it would taste like?' said Johnny.

'The tequila or the worm?' said Lex.

Johnny grinned. 'Both.'

'You are an animal,' Lex said sadly.

Something had been turned inside out and nailed to a display stand. It was still living, still moving. The smell was appalling.

'Why would Hammer want something like that?' said Johnny.

'He's always been attracted to suffering,' said Lex.

'Do you think this was human, originally?' said Annie, staring at the horrid thing with fascinated eyes.

'Hard to tell,' I said. 'I don't recognize any part of it. Is there a sign?'

'No,' said Lex. 'I suppose Hammer didn't need to be reminded of what this is.'

'Can we kill it?' said Annie. 'Put it out of its misery?'

'How?' I said. 'If doing that wasn't enough to kill it, I don't know what would be.'

'We can always try something with fire, on the way back,' said Lex. 'The more I see of Hammer's vault, the more I want to burn the whole place down.'

'Let's wait until we're all out of here first,' said Annie.

Lex smiled briefly. 'Just for you.'

The Ghost came wandering back, and Annie gestured at the inside-out thing.

'Is this the not-dead-not-alive presence you were talking about earlier?'

'No,' said the Ghost. 'What I sensed was much worse.'

My heart almost missed a beat when we rounded the next corner and came face to face with the renowned gentleman adventurer, Dominic Knight. Cool and elegant as always, he'd been stuffed and mounted and carefully posed, like a scarecrow in an immaculate tuxedo.

'How did he come to be here?' said Annie.

'He was shot in the back at the auction,' I said. 'Hammer didn't waste any time collecting him.'

'This is how we'll all end up if they catch us here,' said Annie.

'Speak for yourself,' said the Ghost.

The path suddenly opened out into a clearing, just big enough to hold a menagerie of carefully preserved creatures. A large white horse, with widespread feathered wings. A unicorn, with a long scrolled horn jutting from its forehead. And a manticore, complete with lion's mane and a scorpion's sting that curved over its back. They all smelled strongly of spices and chemicals, and a chill ran through me when I realized they'd all been given the same glass eyes.

'Hammer killed all these wonderful creatures?' said Annie, her voice thick with outrage.

'I doubt he did it himself,' said Lex. 'You'd need a specialist to track creatures this rare.'

'And the only reason Hammer would want them is if they were the last of their kind,' said the Ghost. 'This is so sad.'

'Hammer has had any number of people killed,' said Lex. 'Including you.'

'But I don't matter,' said the Ghost. 'I never mattered to anyone. These were marvels of the age, put on the earth to inspire us. This is like setting fire to a masterpiece, just so you can warm your hands at the flames. It's more than a crime; it's a sin.'

'Save your conscience for the living,' said Lex.

'Can you see their spirits, Ghost?' said Annie. 'Is that why you're so upset?'

He shook his head. 'No. At least Hammer only got their bodies. These spirits of the wild gave up the ghost long ago.'

'Try to hold it together, people,' I said.

I followed the compass needle through yet more narrow

passageways, under towering stacks of the weird and the wonderful, until, finally, we found the television. It stood alone, at the end of a cul-de-sac, a big and bulky old-fashioned set, from the days when the tube took up most of the interior. There was even a heavy wooden surround to help it blend in with the rest of the furniture.

'We had a set like this when I was a child,' Johnny said delightedly. 'It always took ages to warm up.'

'No remote control,' said Annie. 'Just a dial to change the channel, and a few switches.'

'I'm getting that not-dead-not-alive feeling again,' said the Ghost. 'Really strongly now.'

'You think it's connected to the set?' said Lex.

'It must be,' said the Ghost. 'Though I can't see how.'

Annie studied the television carefully, front and back, while being very careful not to touch anything.

'It's not plugged in,' she said finally. 'How are we supposed to test it and make sure it works? Judi Rifkin said she wouldn't pay out a penny unless we could show the thing working, right in front of her.'

'Can't you charm the set into turning itself on?' I said.

Annie frowned. 'I should be able to. But whatever's inside is no technology I'm familiar with.'

I tried the on switch, and the screen glowed pleasantly but remained blank. I tried changing the channel, but it made no difference.

'Shouldn't there be an aerial?' said Lex.

'I don't think it's that kind of television,' said Johnny.

'How do we get it to show us a particular period?' said Annie.

'Ask it nicely?' said Johnny.

I cleared my throat and addressed the television. 'What's happening outside the museum right now?'

The screen immediately showed a view of the cavern floor, still littered with bits and pieces from all the golem guards we'd blown up. It took me a moment to realize we were viewing the scene from above – and a lot higher up than the pylons with their surveillance cameras could have managed. So whose viewpoint were we seeing? I turned the set off.

'That's enough. We know it works, and that's all that matters.

Getting it to do what Judi wants is Judi's problem. Let's get the set out of here.'

'It'll take all of us to carry something that big and awkward,' said Annie. 'And how are we supposed to manoeuvre it through the museum if we have to keep dodging back and forth again?'

Lex picked up the television with no visible effort and stuck it under one arm.

'Now, that is some serious showing off,' said Johnny.

Lex frowned suddenly, looked at the set and put it down again. 'Something about this feels wrong. How is the television supposed to work? What powers it?'

'There's nothing in Sable's journal about that,' I said.

'I'm starting to think there isn't any technology inside that set,' said Annie.

'It was created by a priest,' said the Ghost. 'Maybe it runs on prayers.'

'You still believe in things like that?' said Johnny. 'You sweet, sentimental old spirit.'

The Ghost looked at him coldly. 'Your knowledge of this world might be extensive, but it's still only this world. There is more.'

'Prove it,' said Johnny.

The rest of us tensed, remembering the way the Ghost scared off the poltergeist attack dogs, but he just smiled easily at Johnny.

'You're asking a dead man to explain the mysteries of life?'

Johnny sniffed loudly and turned his attention back to the television. 'Maybe there's nothing inside it apart from a big crystal ball.'

'We don't need to know how it works,' I said. 'We're just here to steal it.'

'I think it does matter,' said Lex. 'I'm feeling . . . something.'

'If I still had a body, I think I'd have goose pimples,' said the Ghost. He knelt down before the set. 'All right, let's have a look inside you and see what's going on.'

He thrust his head through the screen and then immediately jerked it back out again. Shocked and outraged, he rose quickly to his feet, pointing a shaking finger at the television.

'You really need to see what's inside that! Lex, break it open!'

Lex grabbed hold of both sides of the set and tried to pull

them apart, but the heavy wooden surround resisted him. So he armoured his hands in light and darkness, and tore the television apart as though it was made of paper. And inside there was nothing but a severed human head, still alive and aware.

It was a man's head, with a handsome face that seemed familiar, though I couldn't quite place it. The eyes were sad and wise. He smiled at all of us and began to speak in a low calm voice.

'Hello, at last, my dear friends. Lex Talon, who believes himself the Damned. Believe in God, Lex, even if you can't believe in yourself. There is mercy and forgiveness. Johnny Wilde, who thinks he knows the truth but still has trouble telling one illusion from another. Annie Anybody, who has to be so many people, because she's afraid to be herself. The Ghost, who could move on if he really wanted to. And, of course, the man who became Gideon Sable, so he could go back to being who he used to be.

'Thieves and outlaws, all hoping to be better than they are. Welcome. I've been expecting you.'

'Who are you?' I said.

'I am Angelo Montini.'

We all knew that name. The man who could work miracles and performed good works wherever he went. So popular and revered there was a call to make him the Vatican's first living saint.

'You disappeared,' said Annie.

'No,' said Angelo. 'That's not what happened.'

Annie and I looked at each other, remembering the knuckle-bones we saw at the auction.

'Hammer killed you?' I said. 'Why would he want to kill a living saint?'

'Because he's Hammer,' said Lex. 'I killed two angels for that man.'

'No,' said Angelo in his calm, steady voice. 'That's not how I died.'

'I'm sorry we didn't recognize you at first,' said Annie.

He smiled. 'That's all right. You're not seeing me at my best.'

'So Hammer had you kidnapped and then killed?' I said.

'I'm afraid not,' said Angelo. 'My death is one of the few crimes that cannot be laid at his door. It all started when the

Vatican sent a very respected academic priest to prepare me for canonization. Cardinal Rossini, a devout little man, who only wanted to live in peace with his God, as he saw Him. Chosen for his conservative, old-fashioned views, so that if there was any doctrinal reason why I couldn't be sainted, Rossini would be sure to find it. But he came looking for evidence of heresy, of deviation from the true faith. He wasn't prepared to deal with a very different problem. That I had no interest in being a saint.

'The Cardinal was profoundly shocked when he discovered I had no special faith in God. Not even after I discovered I could perform miracles. I lived a normal, healthy life. I loved my food and my wine and my fast cars, and my women . . . So many lovely women. I like to think I was a good man, and I did try to help wherever I could, but I was still only a man.

'The Vatican already knew that; they'd put a lot of effort into hiding it from the world's media. That's why they sent the Cardinal, hoping he'd come up with some doctrinal reason why they wouldn't have to make a man like me a saint. But they should have warned Rossini, instead of just dropping him in the deep end. He was so horrified by what he found that he took matters into his own hands.

'He thought that if the truth got out, it would make his beloved Church a laughing stock. So Rossini said he had a few more questions for me, and when I turned up at his hotel, he invited me inside and stabbed me through the heart. If I'd suspected anything, I think I might have been able to heal even a wound like that, but I never saw it coming.'

He stopped speaking, and we all stared at him for a long while.

'So . . . how did you end up as a television set?' I said finally.

Angelo smiled. 'Questions you never thought you'd hear yourself asking. Rossini turned to old friends, specialists in forbidden knowledge. He brought my body to them and explained the situation. And they used my own powers to turn me into a prophet and a seer – a viewing device for history. Not dead, not alive . . . trapped in a box, watching a world I could never be a part of again. I like to think they didn't really understand what they were doing.

'Rossini said he would present this marvellous new piece of Vatican technology to the world's media and use it to distract them from the sudden disappearance of a living saint. But by then the Cardinal was so traumatized he wasn't thinking clearly. He made such a mess of his presentation that no one believed him. The Vatican quickly cancelled his planned demonstration to avoid further embarrassment, and Rossini was sent somewhere distant and secure. His friends kept their heads down and their mouths shut, and hoped not to be noticed. And I was hidden away in the Holy City's very own Vault of Forbidden Things.'

He smiled reflectively. 'You'd be amazed at what they have in there. Makes this place look like a carnival sideshow. I had some very interesting conversations with some of my fellow incarcerated inconveniences.'

'And then the original Gideon Sable broke in, because he could get into anywhere,' I said. 'He stole the television and sold it to Hammer, so he could use it as a Trojan Horse to get into this vault.'

'Not a technological breakthrough, after all,' said Lex. 'Just the head of a man who was almost a saint, reduced to a collectible.'

'But I still had hope,' said Angelo. 'I knew you were coming.'

'Is there some way we can set you free?' I said.

'Of course,' said Angelo. 'Kill me.'

'You can't ask that of us,' I said. 'We're thieves, not killers.'

Annie looked at me. 'Gideon, please. We can't leave him like this.'

I sighed and nodded slowly. 'Of course we can't. That would be cruel. But . . . how can we kill you, Angelo? I mean, if being stabbed through the heart and having your head cut off didn't do it . . .'

'I could crush his head with my armoured hands,' said Lex.

'Unfortunately, I am protected by my own powers,' said Angelo. 'The men who built this set made sure nothing could destroy me – not even someone like you. Perhaps especially someone like you. They wanted me to go on being useful to the Church for ever. My punishment – for not being the kind of man they thought I should be.'

'There's always a way,' I said steadily. 'If you have the right toys. Like a skeleton key that can unlock anything.'

'I knew you'd get there eventually,' said Angelo.

We all took a moment to say goodbye to him, and then I used the key to unlock his protections, and Lex used his hands of light and darkness to crush the head with one convulsive movement. It was all over very quickly.

'Is he really dead now?' Annie said quietly.

'I can't see his spirit anywhere,' said the Ghost.

Lex looked at the crushed mess in his hands and let it drop to the floor. The armour disappeared from his hands, as though ashamed of what it had been used for.

'I thought there would be blood,' he said. 'I think it might have been easier if there had been blood. I'm used to having blood on these hands.'

'You gave him a gift you've never known, Lex,' said Johnny. 'Peace, at last.'

'OK . . .' I said. 'This heist is now officially over. We've destroyed Hammer's most precious possession, so let's settle for that. Grab anything you like the look of, and then we're out of here.'

Lex looked at me sharply. 'You promised me the immortality drug.'

'I only came here to find something that could put an end to me,' said the Ghost.

'And I still need to find something to help control my gift,' said Annie.

'Actually,' said Johnny. 'I just came along for the ride. It's been such fun!'

'I can't do everything for you!' I said. 'Look around! If you can't find what you want, find something you'll settle for.'

Lex grabbed me by the throat with one hand and lifted me into the air. My feet kicked helplessly as I fought for air. Lex pushed his face right into mine.

'There never was a Santa Clara Formulation, was there?'

'Possibly not,' I said.

Annie moved in beside Lex, although she had enough sense not to try to touch him. 'Please, put him down.'

'Why?' said Lex.

'Because I'm asking you to.'

'He'll cheat you just like he cheated me.'

'He got us this far,' said Annie.

'Check the freezer,' I said, forcing the words out. 'Might be something else in there that you could use.'

Lex thought about it, and then threw me to one side and went back to the freezer. Annie helped me to my feet.

'I did warn you . . .'

'So you did,' I said hoarsely. 'I must learn to keep more of a distance from that man. But who knows, maybe he'll find something better than the formula.'

'Better than immortality?' said Annie. 'You really are an optimist.'

She turned away and reached out with her gift, and strange machines turned themselves on and off all across the vault – showing what they could do, in hope of pleasing her. Some vanished from one shelf and reappeared on another. Some turned themselves into other things. A few even opened fire on each other for hogging Annie's attention. Several sang her a very sweet love song, in pleasant harmonies, until she shouted at them to stop. After that, it was very quiet in the vault.

The Ghost wandered here and there, walking in and out of things, shaking his head sadly. 'I was sure Hammer would have something to kill a ghost. He's killed so many things . . .'

Johnny picked up the odd item here and there, muttered, "Pretty" or "Interesting" and then put them down again.

I checked the list I'd made from Sable's journal and moved quickly back and forth, picking up half a dozen useful items. They were all exactly where the journal said they'd be. One in particular made me smile. I just knew it was going to come in handy.

And that was when Fredric Hammer came storming into the vault, along with a dozen heavily armed guards.

ACT FOUR
End Game

THIRTEEN
The Unexpected
Really

We all spun round, startled, as Hammer made his entrance. He took a good look at us, down the long open passageway that connected us to the vault door, and then smiled mockingly. The straight passage threw me for a moment. I was sure we'd taken all kinds of twists and turns to get this far. Someone had changed the world while I wasn't watching. The others moved in close, to stand with me and stare defiantly back at Hammer.

His smile broadened, as though he knew what we were thinking. He had to be the one responsible for reworking the vault's interior, which suggested he'd changed our surroundings because he knew we were in here. While I was still trying to get my head round that, Lex took a step forward. I spoke to him quickly, without taking my eyes off Hammer.

'You stay right where you are, Lex. We're in no immediate danger. The guards won't dare open fire on us, for fear of hitting the collection.'

'That didn't stop them at the auction,' said Lex.

'That was just stuff he wanted to be rid of. Everything in this vault is the pride of Hammer's collection.'

'What if they come in here after us?' said Annie.

'Then we disappear into the maze of tunnels, split up and take them down in an ambush.'

'He's being optimistic again,' said Johnny.

Hammer raised a hand and snapped his fingers imperiously. And just like that, all the stacks lining the narrow path just vanished. Nothing stood between us and the very heavily armed guards apart from a whole lot of empty space. I gestured urgently for everyone to stand still, but I needn't have bothered. They were all rooted to the spot by shock and surprise. Hammer gestured lazily and his guards fanned out, making sure they could cover all of us with their guns, while still blocking the only way out of the vault. I glanced at the passageways behind us, but you can't hide in a maze if someone can make it all disappear with a snap of their fingers.

If I hadn't had my plan to cling on to, I think I might have been a bit worried.

Fredric Hammer smiled genially at all of us. He looked exactly as he had in Judi Rifkin's old photo: a handsome, casually dressed man in his mid-twenties. I wondered fleetingly if that was down to the immortality drug or a really special portrait in his attic. Of course, if Hammer had owned a portrait like that, he would have flaunted it as part of his collection. It's funny the directions your mind can run off in when you're hanging on to your self-control by your fingernails.

Hammer's smile disappeared as he realized for the first time that we all had some of his possessions in our hands.

'Put those down!' he said loudly. 'All of them. Or I'll have my guards put you down.'

Lex growled dangerously.

'No, Lex,' I said sternly. 'You might have bulletproof armour, but the rest of us don't. The guards would kill every one of us before you could get anywhere near them.'

Lex nodded reluctantly and stayed where he was, scowling fiercely at Hammer. I put down what I was holding, slowly and very carefully, and one by one the others did, too. I raised my hands in the air, and so did Annie. Lex, Johnny and the Ghost didn't. Hammer came striding forward, backed by his guards, and finally stopped a respectful distance away from us. He gestured easily at the open space where his stacks of treasures used to be.

'Don't worry; I can always bring them back. I've gone to a lot of trouble to make sure everything here obeys my will, in all things. Which is, of course, how things should be. Oh, please, put your hands down. It's not like I'm interested in your surrender.'

Annie and I did so, while Hammer looked us over, studying each face carefully in turn as though ticking them off against some mental list. When he was done, he nodded familiarly to the Damned.

'Been a while, hasn't it, Historian? But I always knew we'd get together again. We have so much unfinished business between us. And, of course, you still have something that belongs to me.'

'Go to Hell,' said Lex.

'No, my dear fellow; that's where you're going.'

He turned away to study Johnny, and for the first time I thought I saw uncertainty in Hammer's eyes. Perhaps because Johnny was the only one of us who didn't seem the least bit threatened by the armed guards. He smiled easily at Hammer, who made a point of smiling easily back.

'So, here at last we have the infamous, notorious and entirely unpredictable Wild Card himself. So many adjectives, so little time. Perhaps I should just settle for "annoying". You'll make a splendid addition to my collection. One way or another.'

'And they say *I'm* crazy,' said Johnny. 'Which I'm actually not. It's the world that needs a rewrite.'

Hammer only glanced at me and Annie, before moving on to smile and wave cheerfully at the Ghost, just to make it clear that he could see him. The Ghost glowered back, not least because Hammer didn't seem to recognize him.

Hammer rubbed his hands together briskly and smiled happily on all of us. 'Congratulations! You are the only people ever to break into my private vault. But I'm afraid I have to tell you . . . I always knew you were coming. I saw it on my special television set. In fact, it was the first thing I looked for: to see who'd try to take my treasures away from me. And there you were on the screen, appearing in my cavern and making a mess of my defences, infiltrating my museum and making yourselves at home in my vault. I couldn't change any of that, but I could and did make special preparations for your arrival.'

He stopped and looked at us hopefully, in case we wanted to tell him how clever he'd been. Once it became clear that wasn't going to happen, he pressed on.

'I enjoyed watching you dart back and forth in my house, using all the rooms and corridors I carefully left empty. Avoiding the guards who'd been ordered to avoid you. Apart from that idiot on a cigarette break, and I'll deal with him later. Set him on fire, perhaps; that seems appropriate. We all had a great time, watching you run your little maze for no reason. The hard part was to keep from giggling.'

The original Sable saw the empty rooms and corridors on his television, but he never knew why they were empty. I had to wonder what else he might have misinterpreted.

'That's why no one appeared to hear anything that happened outside,' I said. 'I should have realized; it was because you already knew what was going to happen.'

'I'm actually grateful to you for demonstrating the gaps in my defences,' said Hammer. 'Which I will put right, as soon as I'm finished here.'

'Why didn't you just change your defences and stop us getting in?' said Annie.

'Because I'd seen what you were going to do, I knew how to ambush you in the vault,' said Hammer. 'I didn't want to do anything that might change that.'

'I'd like to say something witty and insightful here, about cause and effect,' said Johnny. 'But it's not as if those gentlemen and I have ever been on speaking terms.'

'The Wild Card,' Hammer said admiringly. 'The joker in the pack, who changes all the rules because he doesn't believe there are any. I never could see beyond this point, on the television. It always shut down the moment you entered the vault. But I get it now . . . Having you around confuses the hell out of Space and Time. Even my special television couldn't cope with that.' He stopped and looked around. 'Where is it, by the way? It should be right here.'

'We destroyed it,' said Annie.

Hammer gaped at her. He hadn't seen that coming. When he was finally able to speak again, his voice was choked with shock and outrage.

'Why would you want to do something like that?'

'To set free the poor soul trapped inside it.'

'But . . . It was my favourite thing! How dare you!'

I smiled at my crew. 'You see? I told you this was the best way to get to him.'

Hammer glared at me. 'This was all your doing! Oh, yes, I know who you are. And I'm not going to call you Gideon Sable, because you're not nearly the legend he was. The things that man found for me, down the years . . . No, I think I'll just call you Thief.' He looked at my crew again and shook his head. 'Such small people, to do so much damage. Like the vandals who brought down civilization because they were incapable of appreciating it.'

'No, that's you,' I said. 'Or you wouldn't leave your precious things just standing around in piles, in a hole in the ground.'

'They belong to me,' said Hammer. 'So I can do anything I want with them. That's the point.' He made himself smile again. 'I may have lost my marvellous television, but now I have you. The famous, the infamous and the rest. I can't wait to make you part of my collection. Properly stuffed and mounted, of course, in a dramatic diorama. If you're very nice to me, I'll make sure you're dead before they start the process.'

Lex stirred ominously beside me. 'I'll see you dead first, Hammer.'

'No, Lex!' I said sharply. 'Hold your peace and hold your ground. This is still my plan, and it isn't over yet.'

Lex looked at me. 'And your plan has worked out so well this far.'

'We're here, aren't we?' I said. 'Have a little faith.'

'You're asking a lot of me,' said Lex.

'Because you're worth it,' I said.

Lex growled under his breath but stood his ground. Hammer clapped his hands delightedly.

'You've tamed the Damned! How on earth did you manage it?'

'By promising him a chance to hurt you,' I said.

'Yes,' said Hammer. 'That would do it. I suppose I should thank you for bringing him back to me. But I don't think I will.' He turned his easy smile on Lex. 'I'm glad you brought me back my halos. I'm going to have such fun with them.'

'You're not worthy to wear them,' said Lex.

Hammer raised an eyebrow. 'And you are? After what you did to get them? Anyway, you always did think too small, Historian. Once the armour is mine, I shall use it to plunder the world.'

'But if you can just take anything you want, where's the fun in that?' I said.

Hammer looked at me. 'I don't understand.'

And I could see that he really didn't.

Johnny stepped forward, clearing his throat importantly, and several of the guards trained their weapons on him. Johnny smiled at them indulgently.

'You've heard of me! How nice. Tell you what, why don't you all open fire? Just to see what would happen. Who knows? I don't.'

'My men only follow my orders,' said Hammer. 'Don't try anything, Mr Wilde. The ammunition in those guns is very special. Cursed bullets, retrieved from the bodies of famous victims, and then soaked in the blood of slaughtered innocents. A bit time-consuming, I know, but if a thing is worth doing . . . And I did want to be sure I had something that would stop the Damned, and you.'

'I love it when people take me seriously,' said Johnny. 'But do you honestly think you can stop me from leaving if I decide to go?'

'If you try anything I don't like the look of, my guards will shoot your friends one by one until you stop doing it,' said Hammer.

'Well,' said Johnny. 'You're no fun. You . . . villain, you.'

Hammer turned his attention back to me.

'Take off that ridiculous mask, Thief. I know who you are. I had completely forgotten about you, and her, until I saw you again on my television. If you hadn't planned this little home invasion, I doubt I'd have ever given you another thought. Oh, by the way, Thief, did you know your little friend was the one who betrayed you the last time you tried to steal from me? Oh, yes . . . She gave you up in a moment, to save her true name. And then I took that from her anyway.'

Annie couldn't bring herself to look at me. I took hold of her chin and made her look.

'I knew it was you,' I said. 'I've always known. Any number of people couldn't wait to tell me – friends and enemies. It didn't matter to me then and it doesn't now. I would have done the same thing.'

'No, you wouldn't,' said Annie. She pulled her chin out of my grasp but made herself meet my gaze. 'This is why I stayed away. Because I couldn't face you after what I did.'

'I forgave you long ago,' I said.

'But I never forgave myself.'

'Then let me do it for you.'

'This is all very sweet,' said Hammer in a long-suffering sort of way. 'But I really don't care. You came here to steal from me, and no one gets away with that. So, Thief, let's make a start by relieving you of all your precious toys. That seems only fair. You can begin by handing over that special pen of yours. I saw you using it on the television. I haven't quite figured out what it is or what it does, but I have people who can do that for me. All that matters is that it's intriguing and I want it. So bring it to me, right now.'

Several guards covered me with their guns as I moved forward. I produced the ballpoint pen from inside my jacket pocket, slowly and carefully, so as not to upset the guards. When I finally came face to face with Hammer, he stuck out a hand for the pen – and I hit the button. Time crashed to a halt, just long enough for me to make one small change. And then I started Time up again. No one noticed anything had happened, because for them nothing had. I kept my gaze down and my shoulders slumped, as though I had no more tricks left in me. Hammer snatched the pen out of my hand, and I tensed, but fortunately he had enough sense not to mess with something he didn't properly understand. He slipped the pen carelessly into his jacket pocket.

'Your other toys can wait,' he said. 'I probably have better versions in my collection anyway. You can go back to the others now.'

I backed away, never taking my eyes off him, and Hammer never took his eyes off me. Once I was back with my crew, Hammer smiled happily.

'Right! This was all your idea, so you get to die first.' He turned to the nearest guard. 'Shoot him.'

The guard aimed his gun at me.

'No!' said Annie.

The guard opened fire, and Johnny Wilde was suddenly standing right in front of me. The bullets hit Johnny so hard they slammed him off his feet and back into my arms. He cried out once, more in surprise than anything else, and we crashed to the floor together. Annie knelt down beside us. My throat was so tight I couldn't say anything. The whole front of Johnny's tweed suit was soaked in blood. He managed a smile for me.

'I finally worked out what's real,' he said. 'The people you care for. Hello. I must be going.'

He stopped breathing. And for the first time, he looked very small and very ordinary.

The Damned was already wrapped in his armour and charging the guards. They all opened fire at once, and every single cursed bullet hit the Damned squarely, but they didn't even slow him down.

Annie and I clung tightly together and kept our heads down. The Ghost stood tall, entirely unmoved as stray bullets passed right through his immaterial form to shatter precious items behind him. His gaze never once left Hammer.

Lex raged among the guards, tearing them limb from limb with awful strength. Terrible tearing sounds were drowned out by horrid screams, as the guards bled and died, but Lex never said a word. His anger was too great for that. He struck them down and threw them aside, until, just a few moments later, Hammer was the only one still standing. All the guards were dead, what was left of them lying scattered in bloody pieces across the floor. Hammer stood there trembling, spattered in his guards' blood, and the Damned turned his back on him. He put aside his armour and came back to kneel beside Johnny's body. He reached out a steady hand and gently closed Johnny's staring eyes.

'Goodbye, my friend. I doubt we'll ever meet again, because if anyone deserves not to end up where I'm going, it's you.'

He took his time getting to his feet again. Annie and I helped each other up, and while we were preoccupied doing that, Hammer went to leave, only to find the Ghost was already standing before the open door, blocking the way. Hammer sneered and went to walk through him, only to stop dead when the Ghost planted a very solid hand on his chest. Hammer fell back, startled.

'Do you remember ordering my death?' said the Ghost.

Hammer quickly regained his composure. 'Oh, yes . . . You're the forger. It was a very good Turin Shroud, I'll give you that.

It fooled me and a lot of my experts. But you can't con all of the people all of the time.' He chuckled briefly. 'I did get a bit annoyed with you, didn't I?'

'You had me killed in such a horrific way I still can't bear to remember it,' said the Ghost.

Hammer shrugged. 'You earned it. And I needed to send a message.'

The Ghost stared at him for a long moment, and Hammer stirred uncomfortably.

'You're looking very well, for a ghost,' he said finally.

'How is it that you're able to see me?'

'I took a potion,' said Hammer. 'So I could enjoy all the ghosts in my collection.'

Lex and Annie and I came forward to confront Hammer. He drew himself up and faced us defiantly.

'You can't kill me,' Hammer said flatly. 'The first thing I looked for on the television was my own future. I'm still very much alive, years from now.'

'I know,' I said. 'That was one of the first things my predecessor looked for when he was setting up this heist.'

'You never told us that,' said Annie.

'Now you know why I was so insistent we could only hurt Hammer, not kill him,' I said.

'You see?' Hammer said triumphantly. 'There's nothing you can do to me.'

The Ghost advanced on Hammer, and he backed away.

'Don't you feel any guilt?' said the Ghost. 'For all the people you hurt and the lives you ruined?'

'What do people matter?' said Hammer. 'Compared with all the precious things in the world? There's never any shortage of people.'

'Our short lives are all that matter,' said the Ghost. 'Because we're a long time dead.'

I closed in on Hammer from his blind side, thrust my hand into his jacket pocket and took back my pen. Hammer fumed but had enough sense not to say anything. I put the pen away, while Hammer did his best to stare us all down.

'More of my guards are on their way. And I have all kinds of personal protection. There's no way you can win!'

'I'm sure I can find one if I try hard enough,' said Lex. 'Why should you live when my good friend is dead?'

'You can't kill him, Lex,' I said quickly.

Lex looked at me angrily. 'Why do you keep saying that? Johnny was one of us!'

'I know,' I said. 'He gave up his life for me.'

'Give me one good reason why I shouldn't kill this piece of garbage,' said Lex. 'The world will smell better once he's gone.'

'You chose to be an agent of the Good,' I said.

'Only to piss off Hell. Anyway, killing a monster like him would be a good thing.'

'But what would Johnny want you to do?' I said.

Lex scowled. 'Something annoying, probably. But he never was vindictive. He always was a better man than me.' He turned his scowl on Hammer. 'I'll make you a deal. Give me the immortality drug and I won't kill you.'

The hope that had flared in Hammer's face at the mention of a deal disappeared again.

'It's all gone,' he said. 'There was only the one dose, and I drank it before Judi could get her hands on it.'

'Then what use are you?' said Lex.

Hammer took in the look on the Damned's face and had to turn his head away.

'Hold off, Lex,' I said. 'I have a use for him.'

'Convince me,' said Lex, his cold gaze fixed on Hammer.

'You don't understand what's going on here,' I said. 'No one does, except me.' I smiled at Hammer. 'This was never your plan, for all your foresight; it was mine. I knew you'd use the television to look ahead in Time, to check for people coming to steal from you. Because that's what I would do. So I gave the matter some thought. How could I get in here, and do what I needed to do, if you knew we were coming? But then I had the idea to make the Wild Card a part of my crew. I knew his unique nature would confuse things wonderfully.'

'And by bringing him here, you got him killed,' said Hammer.

'No,' said Lex. 'That's down to you.'

I turned to the Ghost. 'I promised you an end to your ghostly existence. How would you like a chance at a second life?'

'You think there's something here that could do that?' said the Ghost. 'I looked really hard and I couldn't see anything.'

'That's because I'd already picked it up,' I said. 'Remember the bone ring I told you about, fashioned from one of the possessed Gadarene swine? The one that allows you to possess someone else's body?'

The Ghost was already shaking his head. 'I told you. I won't drive someone else out, just so I can take their body for myself. I won't do that.'

'Not even Fredric Hammer?' I said.

The Ghost turned slowly to look at Hammer.

'Sable's journal said the possessing ring was here,' I said. 'I slipped it into my pocket earlier, when no one was looking. And when Hammer demanded I hand over my pen, that allowed me to get close enough to quietly slip the ring on to his finger.'

Hammer looked down at his hand and made a shocked sound. He tried to pull the ring off, but it wouldn't budge.

I nodded to the Ghost. 'Take Hammer's body. Take his whole life – for your revenge.'

'Love to,' said the Ghost.

He walked forward and disappeared inside Hammer. The man cried out once, and then his voice cut off abruptly. His eyes were suddenly kind, and when he smiled, there was none of Hammer's malice in it. He took a deep breath and stretched slowly, like a cat, savouring it.

'I'm alive again. I can feel again! I'm back.'

I turned to Lex. 'And that is why I couldn't let you kill Hammer.'

Lex shook his head slowly. 'You couldn't just tell me?'

'Not until it was time. I couldn't be sure who was listening.'

'But if that's the Ghost in Hammer's body,' said Lex, 'where has Hammer's spirit gone?'

'Where he should have gone long ago,' I said. 'Where he deserves to be. I promised you revenge on Hammer, Lex. Have I delivered?'

Lex looked at the Ghost, smiling his gentle smile with Hammer's face.

'It'll do,' said Lex.

I smiled at Annie. 'This heist was never just about burgling

Hammer's vault. It was about getting some personal justice for all of us. Happy now?'

'I'm getting there,' said Annie.

Lex nodded to the Ghost in Hammer. 'Welcome back to the world. What will you do with your new life?'

'Enjoy all the good times that Hammer cheated me out of,' said the Ghost. 'And then I think I'll put his life to some real use. With all his money and resources, I can finally help the people I always wanted to.'

'And the collection?' said Annie.

'I think I'll sell it all off,' the Ghost said cheerfully. 'Or destroy it, if need be.'

'Will Hammer's people let you do that?' said Lex.

'I imagine they're used to obeying his orders, whether they make sense or not,' said the Ghost.

'I got what I came here for,' said Lex. 'Hammer is dead. Shame about the immortality drug.' He looked at me. 'You lied to get me here. But I suppose I would have done the same thing in your position.'

'Does that mean I'm forgiven?' I said.

'I'm still working on that,' said Lex.

Annie moved to stand between us. 'To get to him, you'd have to go through me.'

'Then I'd better forgive him,' said Lex.

And then we all looked round, startled, as Johnny Wilde leapt to his feet, laughing out loud in sheer exuberance. He checked the front of his suit, sticking his fingers in the bullet holes and grinning at the blood. He danced around the vault, jumping up and clicking his heels together, until he finally crashed to a halt before us, beaming happily.

'I'm the Wild Card, remember? Too weird to live, too strange to die!'

Lex laughed, catching us all by surprise, and pulled Johnny into a bear hug.

'I thought I'd lost you!'

'You see,' said Johnny. 'You *can* care about someone other than yourself.'

'Oh, shut up and let me enjoy the moment, you annoying little weirdo.'

I had to ask. 'Johnny, when you got between me and that guard, did you know those bullets couldn't kill you?'

'Of course,' he said. 'Sort of. Maybe.'

'Who would have thought it?' said the Ghost. 'Justice and good times for everyone. I never thought I'd live to see the day . . .'

Annie looked at me thoughtfully. 'You promised me I'd find something here to give me back control over my gift.'

'You already have it,' I said. 'The problem was never with the gift, but with your lack of self-confidence. Haven't you noticed how your control returned as we worked the heist?'

Annie smiled and shook her head. 'You always were that little bit sneakier than me.'

'Hearing you say that makes all of this worthwhile,' I said. 'So, where do we go from here?'

'Anywhere we want,' said Annie.

I took her in my arms, and we kissed the missing years away. After a while, the others started making impatient noises, and we broke apart.

'Just like old times,' I said to Annie.

'Oh, I think we can do better than that,' said Annie.

'I set this up so we could make enough money to leave our old lives behind,' I said. 'We won't get our millions from Judi Rifkin now, but we can still walk out of here with as many precious things as we can carry.'

'Sounds like a plan to me,' said Annie.

'And then we can live happily ever after – if that's what you want.'

'Yes,' said Annie. 'I'd like that.'

We all looked round as Lex picked up the massive freezer as though it weighed nothing.

'You said we could take anything we could carry . . .'

'Show off,' said Johnny.

FOURTEEN
And Finally

The Ghost as Hammer ordered his security people to let us go, and they did. He escorted us back out into the cavern, already full of plans for how best to use his new position to atone for past sins. He stood outside the museum and waved us goodbye as we made our way across the open cavern floor.

Back in the Perfect Pizza Palace, Lex and Johnny dumped the freezer in a corner and dropped down at the nearest empty table. They ordered everything on the menu and launched into a spirited discussion on what they were going to do with their new lives, while everyone else tried hard to pretend that they weren't eavesdropping. Annie and I left them to it.

Outside, the car was gone, so we walked off into the night, hand in hand.

Because the best thing you can steal . . . is a second chance to get things right.

CPSIA information can be obtained
at www.ICGtesting.com
Printed in the USA
LVHW091943140621
689203LV00005B/2/J

9 780727 891228